JOSS

BY ERIN FALLIGANT

★ American Girl®

Published by American Girl Publishing

20 21 22 23 24 25 26 QP 10 9 8 7 6 5 4 3 2 1

Illustrations by Maike Plenzke
Cover image by Maike Plenzke · Book design by Gretchen Becker

Cataloging-in-Publication Data available from the Library of Congress

americangirl.com/service

FOR MY MOTHER,
WHO TAUGHT ME TO ALWAYS
BE TRUE TO MYSELF—ONE
HUNDRED PERCENT

—E.F.

Dylan & Nico

Reina & Liam

Be all in. 100%

Coach Kara

Tina Hart

YOU GO GIRL!

Surfing TOURNAMENT 2020

Chasing the Sun

Wax

Sunscreen

WiTH GRATiTuDe To:

Crystal da Silva, who holds multiple shortboard titles, including the 2007–2008 Sun Diego Surf Women's Pro-Am division and the 2009 and 2013 World Deaf championships: for being a guiding light for Joss's surfing experience.

Dr. Sharon Pajka, professor of English at Gallaudet University: for her invaluable insights regarding portrayals and perceptions of deaf characters in adolescent literature.

Julie Petersen and Sara Jo Moen, owners of Fury Athletics of Madison, Wisconsin, whose competitive cheer teams have won many prestigious competitions: for their guidance about all things cheer—including the bow!

Jennifer Richardson, AuD, educational audiologist and founder of Hearing Milestones: for her extensive contributions in matters of Joss's hearing loss, accommodations, communication, and social and emotional experiences.

Bianca Valenti, professional big-wave surfer and cofounder of the Committee for Equity in Women's Surfing: for her expertise in surf culture and for making the world of surfing a better place for all women and girls.

CONTENTS

A Perfect Wave
CHAPTER 1

*N*ever *turn your back on the ocean.* That's a surfer's number one rule, because the water is always changing. Every day, it's different. Every *hour*, it's different. Look away, and you might miss a killer wave—or get pummeled by one.

Or the ocean might be resting—taking a snooze between sets of waves. That's the time to paddle out, before the next set comes through.

As soon as I sensed the ocean falling asleep, I paddled like crazy through the foamy white water, belly on my board and head up. My arms cut through the surf, stronger and faster with each stroke. I *had* to get to deeper water to catch one last wave this afternoon.

When the next wave came, I dove into it instead of over it. I grabbed the rails, or sides, of my board and pushed down, plunging face-first into the water. It's called a duck dive, but I felt more like a dolphin, tunneling through the white water to get to the peaceful world below the waves. Then, as soon as the wave passed, I surfaced, ready to paddle again.

When a surfer caught a wave up ahead, I veered left, steering clear of her path. Sofia! My best friend was easy to spot. In her coral swim top and lime-green board shorts, she stood out like a wild parrot in a flock of gray gulls.

We call ourselves Surf Sisters, even though we don't look like sisters. Sofia wears her shiny black hair in an edgy bob, and my brown hair falls every which way over my shoulders. We're different kinds of surfers, too. I'm the speed demon who attacks waves like they're skateboard ramps, trying to catch air. Sofia is more graceful and does lots of tech tricks. But that girl has some serious skills—she can rip.

I watched her cut back and forth in a figure eight, dancing with the water until the wave fizzled out. She waved at me and rode the white water back to shore.

Your turn, I told myself. *Get out there and show what you can do!*

After a few more strokes, I reached the lineup, the calm part of the ocean past the white water where you sit on your board and wait for the perfect wave. My brother Liam and a few other surfers bobbed up and down on their boards, staring toward the open water.

Liam is eighteen and working on going pro. He's already sponsored by Sofia's mom's board shop, where he works. But he wants to get a major sponsor, and I know he will someday. Liam knows exactly where to sit to catch the best waves.

Sure enough, he had his eye on a peeler—a wave breaking gradually along its length, like a zipper closing. I held my breath, waiting. But he didn't take the wave! Instead, he pointed toward me as if to say, *It's all yours.*

Yes! I didn't waste a second. When a perfect wave comes, you go for it. You have to be all in—one hundred percent—just like pro surfer Tina Hart says.

I turned my board to face the beach and paddled like mad, trying to get ahead of the wave. *You've got this*, I told myself. *Go!*

But before I could pop up on my board, someone beat me to the wave.

I glanced over my shoulder just in time to see my other, way more annoying brother hop to his feet and steal my wave. *Dylan.* He knows the rule—one surfer per wave, for safety's sake. But Dylan's not big on following rules. He's pretty much fourteen going on four.

"That's *my* wave!" I shouted.

I've been surfing the Break—our favorite surf spot in Huntington Beach—since I was six, but sometimes Dylan acts like I don't belong here. Like every wave is his to steal, and girls like me should stay on the beach and cheer him on.

It's my ocean, too! I wanted to holler after him. But it wouldn't make any difference.

Dylan had been extra full of himself ever since he rode through the tunnel of a barreling wave a couple of weeks ago. I mean, it was a *mini* tube—it wasn't like he stood up all the way inside it. He caught the trick with the camera attached to his board, but when I watch the video, all I notice are my brother's knobby knees.

Anyway, this wave—*my* wave—was no barrel. And Dylan caught it way too late. The only trick he managed to pull off was a goofy frog dive before going over the falls.

"Ha!" I cried, slapping the water. "Serves you right." Then I spun back around—just in time to get caught off-guard by a sneaker set of waves. I tumbled over the falls, too, swallowing a mouthful of salt water. *Blech.* I surfaced, my throat burning, and paddled back to the lineup.

When my wave finally came, I popped up on my board, my heart racing. Anything can happen out here on the water—no two waves are ever the same. But I was ready.

I carved across the face of the wave, pumping my legs to build speed. *This* is my happy place. *This* is where I belong. Not on the beach, but out here, flying across the water. I, Jocelyn Elizabeth Kendrick, have a need for speed.

As I reached the bottom of the wave, I turned and pumped back up. I imagined that I was pro surfer

Tina Hart, about to wow the crowd with one of her famous aerials. *Get ready to fly!* I told myself.

I almost launched off the wave—well, the nose of my board caught some air anyway. Instead, I did a quick snap, spraying water behind me. I could almost hear my imaginary fans on the beach go wild!

But *uh-oh*. The rail of my board caught in the water. And I was going down.

Instead of falling backward into the soft foam, I landed hard in the flats, or front of the wave. I plunged off my board into the churning water. *Smack!* The water stung my bare skin.

As I tumbled down through the water, my pride stung, too, because I'd just pulled a Dylan. I'd spent so much time wowing my imaginary crowd that I'd lost my focus—and totally messed up my trick.

I slid back onto my board, belly first. As I rode the waves in, I saw Dylan waving from shore, pointing at his phone and laughing. He'd recently bought a new camera lens that connects to his phone, making it easier to film surf tricks. And, ugh—from the looks of it, he'd recorded every second of my wipeout.

When I reached shallow water, I made a beeline for my towel, dodging a sand castle, a few sunbathers, and the patchwork of beach towels strewn across the sand. *Sheesh.*

It was only the first weekend of May, but already the beach was crowded.

When Dylan hollered something, I didn't strain to hear him. I was born deaf in my left ear. I can hear a little with my right, at least when I wear my hearing aid. But I can't wear it in the water, and I hadn't put it back in yet. So I pointed to my right ear and signed, "It's too loud," in American Sign Language, or ASL. The surf *was* really loud, but it was also an excuse to ignore Dylan's trash talk. I shrugged as if to say, *Sorry, bro.* Then I turned away before he could sign something back. It's one of my best little-sister survival skills.

As I set down my board next to Sofia's, I felt a prick of envy. Sofia's mom owns the SoCal Board Shop, so Sofia is always sporting the newest board. But I was stuck with Dylan's hand-me-down shortboard—dings and all—at least until I'd saved enough of my allowance for a new one.

When I reached for my towel, I spotted a message that Sofia had left for me in the sand: a cluster of shells and stones in the shape of an arrow.

Sofia is forever beachcombing. When she isn't picking up litter, she's collecting seashells, stones, and other treasures and turning them into tiny works of art. But an arrow? What was that all about? It pointed up the beach toward the board shop.

Aha! My Surf Sister was probably telling me she'd been struck by a snack attack.

I quickly dried my ear and popped in my hearing aid. *Ugh. Sand.* I hate the gritty feeling in my ear. But as a surfer, I'm pretty much always tracking sand somewhere—on my feet, in my hair, or even in my shorts pockets.

I hopped up to find Sofia. Luckily, Dylan had moved on to his next target. He was filming his buddy Nico attempting a headstand on his board. Nico is one of the bravest surfers at the Break. He'll try any trick, but he usually can't land it. Sure enough, he toppled sideways into the waves. When his dark curly head popped out of the water, he pumped his fist in the air.

I'd barely made it past the weathered blue lifeguard tower when I saw Sofia racing toward me, waving a colorful sheet of paper. When she got closer, she thrust it into my hands.

"Read this!" Her dark eyes flashed. "My mom just . . ." I strained to catch her last words, but the roar of the surf drowned them out.

"Your mom did what?" I asked, watching her lips as she repeated herself.

"She just posted it in the shop. Read it!"

I read the flyer in about ten seconds flat:

SURF THE COAST • SAVE THE COAST

Video Contest

Submit a video showing what you love—and want to protect—about your favorite surf spot. Winners will receive new boards from SoCal Board Shop and a surf session with pro surfer

⋟TINA HART!⋞

Video submissions due June 14.
Team entries encouraged!
Winners will be announced following a beach cleanup at Huntington Beach Pier on International Surfing Day, **Saturday, June 20.**

"Whoa." I could barely breathe. "Tina Hart is actually coming here?"

Sofia danced on her toes. "Yes! She's probably judging the video contest, too. She's all about saving the . . ."

She turned away for a second, so I didn't hear every word. (Sometimes when Sofia gets excited, she forgets that I need her to face me when she speaks.) But I got the gist. I knew Tina had founded Save the Coast, an organization that cleans up beaches and protects sea animals. I mean, as if her surf skills weren't cool enough! Tina is always featured in women's surfing magazines. She can surf better than most boys here at the Break. Not even Dylan would drop in on her wave.

"I've wanted to meet her for like forever," breathed Sofia.

I nodded. "I know. I pretty much want to *be* her." As I read the flyer again, my heart raced. "Sofia, we *have* to do this!"

"You and Sofia have to do *what*?" Dylan asked, popping up from out of nowhere. He shook the mop of hair out of his eyes and glanced at the flyer. Then he swooped in like a seagull, grabbed the flyer, and tore off down the beach, waving the piece of paper like a victory flag.

"Hey!" I shouted.

Sofia grabbed my arm so I wouldn't try to chase him. "Don't worry," she said, laughing. She pulled a second folded flyer from her pocket.

"That's my Surf Sister, always thinking ahead," I said, throwing my arm around her shoulder. "Let's grab our boards. We've got a video to make."

We finally had the chance to meet Tina Hart. To *surf* with her! And like I said, when a perfect wave comes, you have to go for it.

I was all in—one hundred percent.

Bulldog on a Board

CHAPTER 2

W hat do you love about the Break?" I asked Sofia.
"That's what our video is supposed to show."

It was Sunday morning, and I'd spread out my towel on the sand with Sofia to my right so I could hear her over the noisy surf. But she was busy moving stones around in the sand. "Earth to Sofia! We're supposed to be working on our video, remember?" I gave her a nudge.

"I am [*mumble, mumble*]," she said.

"What?" I asked.

"Sorry," she signed, and glanced up so I could see her face as she spoke. "I said I *am* working on our video. Making art helps me think." She sat back to show me her masterpiece: a seal made of smooth dark stones, with green sea glass for an eye and twigs for whiskers.

"That's *so* cute!" I said. "So what you love about the Break is making adorable sea animals out of rocks?"

She grinned. "Pretty much. But ... ew!" She dug a plastic bottle cap out of the sand. "I *don't* love trash. Don't people know animals eat this stuff, thinking it's food?"

I held out the trash bag we always bring to the beach,

but she held up a finger, telling me to wait. Then she positioned the bottle cap above her seal's nose like a beach ball and snapped a quick photo before throwing the cap away. Leave it to creative Sofia to turn trash into treasure.

"How do you come up with this stuff?" I asked.

She shrugged. "The Break inspires me. Do you think we could use my art in the video?"

"Yes!" I said. "Tina Hart would be all over that seal. She loves animals as much as you do."

"So what do *you* love best about the Break?" Sofia asked.

I spun my bracelet around my wrist, thinking. Sofia had made matching bracelets for us as a reminder that we're Surf Sisters, and I never take mine off. *Making art helps me think*, Sofia had said. And her bracelet helped *me* think whenever I needed to come up with a good idea.

As I stared out at the water, I caught Liam doing a frontside air, launching off the wave and catching serious air before landing. That gave me an idea. "Trying new tricks!" I announced. "That's what I love. The tricks Liam taught me to do—and the ones I'll learn someday."

I knew Tina Hart would understand what I meant. She grew up in Huntington Beach, too, and used to surf the Break all the time. When she was ten—like I am now—she landed her first frontside air here. Somebody posted a video of it online, and I've watched it about a thousand times.

But how am I going to show Tina what I can do? I wondered. *Should I film my best tricks?*

Sofia waved to get my attention. "So our video will show my art and your surf tricks?"

I nodded. It was a start anyway. I jumped up and brushed the sand off my legs. "Do you want to film me now?" I gestured toward the perfect waves. "Surf's up!"

"Um, *yeah.*" She hopped up and held out her fist. "Ready?"

We bumped fists. We turned sideways and bumped hips. We whirled around and bumped our other hips. Then we bumped fists again and "blew it up," spreading our fingers as if we'd caused a ginormous explosion.

Then I popped out my hearing aid and tucked it in its case under my towel. This girl was ready to *rip.*

"Let me see!" I scooted closer to Sofia on the towel as she scrolled through her videos. "Did you catch my floater?"

Liam had taught me how to get past crumbly parts of waves. I could catch the face of the wave, slide across the foamy top, and then come back down. Floaters felt like gliding—the next best thing to doing airs.

"Here!" Sofia pointed. She pressed PLAY.

I squinted. "Sofia, that's not a floater. And, wait . . . that's not even *me*."

Her face fell. "Oh." She scrolled again. "How about this one?" She'd caught me doing a snap off the top of the wave, but I was really tiny in the video.

"Maybe try zooming in next time?" I said gently.

Sofia bit her lip. "I *did* zoom in on that clip."

A shadow spilled over the phone screen. Dylan stood over us, carrying his board. He waved at me. "Time to go home, Joss."

"No way. Liam's still here!" I pointed toward the water.

"He's working at the board shop this afternoon," he explained, signing as he spoke. "Mom said you get to come home with me, your favorite brother. You're so lucky."

I sighed. "Sorry, Sofia."

I packed up my things and followed Dylan toward the surfboard rack outside the board shop. Sofia's mom lets us lock up our boards there so we don't have to bring them home every night. While Dylan detached the camera from his board, I was struck with a genius idea. If we could borrow Dylan's camera equipment, Sofia and I could finally take some decent videos!

But asking Dylan for a favor is about as much fun as weeding Mom's rock garden. He never gives away anything for free—I'd probably have to do his chores for a month.

I biked after him up Beach Boulevard toward our house in Fountain Valley. When we reached our driveway, I took a deep breath. "Dylan?"

He took off his helmet and shook out his hair. "Yeah?"

I leaned over my handlebars. "Could Sofia and I borrow one of your camera lenses from your phone? Just for like a day—to film clips for the video contest?"

I regretted the question instantly, because Dylan didn't even think about it. "Nope," he said. "Not gonna happen. Nico and I need it for [*scratch, scratch*]."

"Wait, what?" I took off my own helmet, which was brushing against my hearing aid.

"I said Nico and I need it for our own video, which is going to be epic."

Frustration lit a fire in my chest. Before I could respond, our English bulldog, Murph, bounded out of the garage, dragging an old skateboard in her mouth.

"Want to skate, girl?" Dylan asked.

As soon as he set up the board, Murph climbed on. Dylan had spent the last year teaching her how to skateboard and surf. She was a natural! And she was goofy-footed like me, pushing with her left paw and rolling with her right paw forward.

But as she shifted her weight,

the board veered left. *Uh-oh.* For a few feet, Murph rode nose down and tail up. She was pulling off the perfect nose manual, a wheelie done on the front wheels of the skateboard instead of the back. Then she righted herself and hopped off the board.

I laughed—I couldn't help myself. Then I wheeled my bike into the garage, where Dad was leaning over his workbench. He looked up and waved.

"You have sawdust in your eyebrows," I pointed out.

He wiped his face. "That's why I shave my head. To keep the sawdust out." He winked.

In his free time, Dad does woodworking. Lately, he's been turning an old surfboard into a coffee table, which is the closest he comes to surfing. He sinks like a rock in water—not like Mom, who grew up here and has surfed her whole life.

"Want to help?" Dad asked. He gestured toward his surfboard project.

I shook my head. "I can't. I have to research how to film a surf video."

Just mentioning the video made me mad at Dylan all over again, but I let it go. Sofia and I would find a way to film our own epic video without Dylan's fancy camera equipment.

When Murph waddled into the garage dragging her

skateboard, I smiled. *If a bulldog can learn to skate*, I decided, *Sofia and I can figure out how to make a decent video!*

I woke up Monday morning to the smell of dog breath.

Murph was panting in my face, telling me that my phone alarm was vibrating. I keep the phone in my pillowcase so I can feel the alarm going off, but Murph is my backup, which is super sweet and helpful. I just wish her "help" wasn't so stinky.

"Thanks, girl," I said, pushing her snout away.

But I didn't get up right away. And I didn't check the surf report online, which I usually do to see if the waves at the Break will be good for after-school surfing. Nope, this morning, I kept my eyes closed for some quiet time, or what I like to call "QT." Early in the morning or late at night, when I don't have my hearing aid in, I can tune out the world and make everything go quiet—or *almost* quiet.

Voices and sounds drifted down the hall from the kitchen. But they all blurred together, like the blue-green ocean water. Like a swirly backdrop to my thoughts.

QT is the perfect time to imagine my surf tricks. Liam calls it "visualization." He says that imagining yourself doing tricks helps prepare your body to actually do them.

So I pictured myself pulling off the perfect floater: I caught the face of a wave, slid across the top, and rode it back down.

But why stop there?

I did the trick again, except this time I imagined Tina Hart surfing beside me. We split the peak—Tina rode to the left side of the wave and I went right. And when she geared up for a frontside air, I did, too. Why not?

I could almost feel the wind on my face as I pictured myself kicking the tail of the board down and launching off the wave. I hung frozen in the air and then eyed up my target on the wave below. *Yes!* A perfect landing!

When I opened my eyes, Tina Hart smiled at me from the poster on my wall. She had one hand on her hip and the other holding her surfboard. And her expression read, *Whatcha got, girl? Bring it!*

What I had was a new idea for our video, a trick that would make it stand out: the frontside air! Tina Hart had done it when she was my age. So ... could I do it, too? The question washed over me like the tide.

If I could pull off a halfway decent frontside air in our video, Tina Hart would see me—really see me. And Sofia and I would have a pretty good shot at winning the video contest and meeting her face to face.

As my stomach flip-flopped with excitement, Mom flicked the light switch on and off to get my attention.

She was still in her bathrobe, her hair sticking up from sleep. Mom works as a physical therapist, but she takes Monday mornings off. "Breakfast?" she asked, signing the word.

I shook my head. "Not hungry."

Mom gave me her stern look. "Eggs?" she signed. "Cereal?"

"Cereal's faster," I mumbled. I needed to get going so I could talk to Sofia about our video.

I popped in my hearing aid, which I keep in a case by my bed—safe from Murph, who chewed one to bits once. Then I quickly got dressed. As I brushed my hair, I thought of Tina Hart's slogan: *Be all in. 100%.*

If I was going to learn a frontside air in just a month and a half, I had to give it one hundred percent. I took a deep breath and then reached out to give Tina Hart a fist bump before heading out the door.

The Bet

I dragged my foot to stop my skateboard in front of the school. Then I checked to make sure Sofia was behind me.

Whenever we skate, I practice surf tricks, because some of them are easier to learn on a skateboard. The ground below my wheels never shifts—not like waves, which are always changing. And this morning, I had a special trick in store for Sofia.

As I skated toward the curb, I crouched low, kicked the tail of my board down, and popped an ollie, catching air with my board glued to my feet. I landed with a *clack* on the sidewalk. *Score!*

Had Sofia seen? Sure enough, when she caught up to me, she mouthed the word *wow*. She gave me a high five and said, "You're the only girl I know who can . . ."

"What?" I took off my helmet.

"You're the only girl I know who can catch serious air on flat ground," she repeated.

Yes! Now was the perfect time to tell Sofia about the frontside air, which was pretty much an ollie on the water.

But before I could say anything, she pulled out her phone. "Check out the art I made after you left the Break yesterday." She showed me a photo of a dolphin outlined with shells. When I saw the broken comb she'd used for a dorsal fin, I laughed.

"What?" she asked. "What's so funny?"

I pointed to the comb. "You're cleaning up the beach and creating art at the same time."

"Well, yeah!" she said, putting her hand on her hip. "If people see plastic in my art, it'll remind them to stop trashing the beach and hurting animals. Tina will like that, don't you think?"

"She will!" I said. "Good idea."

Then Sofia zoomed in on her art. She'd written a word in the sand inside the dolphin: COURAGE. She shot me an excited glance. "Maybe we can film a word, like *courage*, and then show video of a brave surf trick. Or *friendship*, and show video of us surfing together. That way we combine art and surfing. Cool, right?"

"Yes!" But I knew how to make it even cooler. "What if for the brave surf trick, I pull off a frontside air?"

Sofia laughed out loud. "Yeah, right." When she saw that I was serious, she bit her lip. "That'd be awesome. But ... *can* you do it?"

I wasn't loving the doubt in her eyes. "Not yet. But

we've got a month and a half before the contest deadline. Besides, I only have to land it once for the video."

Sofia shrugged. "True. But it's a really tough trick. And didn't it take you two months just to learn the floater?"

Ouch. I didn't know she'd been keeping track.

She cocked her head. "Anyway, our video isn't going to be about just one trick, right? It'll show lots of words and tricks."

I hesitated. I wasn't as crazy about this idea as she was. I mean, the video was supposed to be about surfing, not art, right? But I just said, "Yeah, we'll do lots of different tricks. And your beach-art words will be cool."

Sofia grinned. "Thanks." She glanced toward the school. "Oops, there's the bell."

I couldn't hear the high-pitched bell, but I followed Sofia toward the door. I wanted to stay positive about our video, but no matter how awesome her beach art was, I wasn't sure those words plus a few basic surf tricks would be enough to win.

I *had* to land the frontside air—and Sofia needed to get it on video! But would there be enough time for me to learn the trick *and* for Sofia to become an expert filmmaker?

Tuesday afternoon at the Break, I moved my phone left and right, looking for Sofia in a sea of gray waves. How was I supposed to track her on that tiny screen? Wait, there she was! Taking a roller coaster ride on a wave. Bottom turn, top turn, bottom turn . . .

I'd offered to film Sofia for our video, thinking that maybe I had some secret camera skills. But just as she did a snap, spraying water behind her, the phone slipped through my sweaty fingers. *No!*

By the time I'd wiped all the sand off the screen, Sofia was jogging out of the waves. "Did you get my roller coaster?" she asked.

"Some of it, but . . . not the last part." I replayed the clip, which ended with a shot of the blue sky and then my worried face filling the frame.

"Ha!" Sofia made me play it again. "Okay, you're fired from filming. My turn."

She grabbed her own phone and sent me out into the water. But half an hour later, Sofia was the one looking like she wanted to dig a hole in the sand and crawl into it.

Her first video showed me carving across the wave— until I surfed right out of the picture. The next one showed me doing cutbacks, like figure eights. At least I *think* it was me. Sofia zoomed in with her fingertips, but I was just a speck in a sea of blue. And the last one was so blurry that

I couldn't tell where the wave ended and my board began.

I sighed. Without Dylan's camera equipment, how could we get any good clips? I was fresh out of genius ideas.

As I gazed at the waves, hoping for inspiration, I spotted Nico lying on his board as it sailed down a wave. His arms were crossed over his chest. Was he taking a *nap*?

Dylan was filming him from shore. *Great*. He was probably getting stellar video.

When Nico sat up on his board and rode it off the wave, Dylan burst out laughing. "Sick, dude!" he shouted. "I got it!" A few teenagers sprawled out on beach towels started cheering, too.

I waved Dylan over. "Can I see the video?"

He held out his phone to show me. The video was so clear and close-up that I felt as if I was in the water with Nico. Dylan was great at tracking him, too.

Too bad he won't film our video, I thought.

Or would he? I hadn't asked that question yet. Maybe if I buttered him up with compliments, he'd throw me a bone.

"That's a really good shot," I said. "I mean, you're pretty much the best filmer here at the Break. Just so you know."

Dylan stared at me as if I had two heads. Sofia did, too.

"Okay," Dylan said slowly, "what do you want, Joss?" His eyes narrowed.

Shoot—he was on to me.

"Want?" I asked innocently. "Nothing really. Oh, but here's an idea," I said, as if I'd just thought it up. "You could film Sofia and me for our contest video! Just a couple of clips—since, you know, you're so good."

He shook his head. "Nah. You and Sofia should do your own thing. Leave the serious filming to us boys." He puffed out his chest in a joking way, but his words stung.

Behind him, I noticed the Surfers Code posted on the lifeguard tower. I could read the first line of the list of rules, written in all caps: GIVE RESPECT TO GET RESPECT.

I snorted. *So much for that.* "C'mon, Sofia." I grabbed my board and headed toward the board shop, hoping Liam was there. Sometimes when I'm in a lousy mood, my oldest brother is the only one who can get me out of it.

When we pushed open the door, Sofia's mom popped up from behind a clothing rack.

"Hi, Ms. Goto," I said.

She waved at us with a hanger in her hand.

"New rash guards?" cried Sofia. "Cool!" She raced over to see the box of swim tops her mom was unpacking, while I scanned the shop for Liam.

There he was, hanging out with his girlfriend, Reina—who also happens to be Nico's older sister.

She waved. "Hey, Joss!"

Reina has Nico's dark hair and golden-brown skin, and for some reason, she always smells like lemons. She's super friendly, but I never know what to say to her.

"Hey," I said back. I figured it was a good start.

"Got a repair job for me?" Liam asked, pointing at my board. He was wearing his orange SoCal Board Shop shirt, which meant he was officially on the job.

I scanned my board for a ding he could fix with resin. There were plenty of them. Dings let water in, making surf-boards feel heavy—like my mood right now.

When I pointed out a ding, Liam grabbed some sand-paper and got to work. That's when I sighed—one of those super loud sighs that no one can ignore.

Liam stopped sanding. "What's up, Joss? Spill it."

So I told him what was on my mind. "Sofia and I are working on our contest video, but Dylan won't film us. And I don't think any of the tricks I can do will impress Tina Hart. I want to do a frontside air, but I don't know if I can."

"That's a tough trick," agreed Liam. "But you've [*scritch-scratch, scritch-scratch*]."

I put my hand on his so he'd stop sanding. "What?"

"Sorry. I said you've mastered tough tricks before. Plus, you're really good at ollies on your skateboard, so you'll figure out the frontside air, too. You just can't do it *yet*." He grinned.

"Thanks, Liam." I suddenly felt lighter. "I just hope I can land it in time for the video contest deadline."

I felt a tap on my shoulder, and then Dylan stuck his big mug in my face. "Are you still talking about the video contest?" he asked. "Give it up, Joss. You're already looking at the winners."

When he threw his arm over Nico's shoulder, Nico shot me an apologetic smile. He was a whole lot nicer than Dylan. I'd do a brother swap with Reina any day.

Reina hopped off her stool and came to stand beside me. "If you and Sofia ever get tired of hanging out with these clowns, you should come try cheerleading with me and my crew," she said with a smile.

Yikes, said a voice in my head. *Did she say cheerleading?* I knew Reina was a cheerleader, and that was fine for her. But for me? *Um, no, thanks.*

Sofia stood up from behind a clothing rack, her eyebrows raised sky-high. I knew my Surf Sister wouldn't be caught dead dancing around a gym either, waving pom-poms and cheering on a bunch of boys.

Reina caught my eye again. "Tryouts are next Monday. You and Sofia would be great at cheer!"

Not a chance, I wanted to say. *Sofia and I are* real *athletes. We're surfer girls—one hundred percent.* But Reina was just trying to be nice, and I didn't want to hurt her feelings.

Luckily, Sofia spoke up for both of us. "Thanks, Reina. We'll probably stick with surfing, though." I almost hugged her—seriously.

"Joss doing cheerleading?" Dylan smirked at me. "I'd pay money to see that. In fact, I'll give you ... twenty bucks if you try out and make it." He licked his thumb and pretended to count a wad of bills.

I don't usually back down from Dylan's dares. But cheerleading? That's where I drew the line—until an idea began to form in my mind ...

"Do I actually have to join the team?" I asked.

He cocked his head. "Nah. I wouldn't make my little sister do something *that* horrible."

"Hey!" Reina swatted his arm. "Not nice."

Dylan darted away, laughing. "So? What do you say, Joss?"

That's when I sprang it on him. "Keep your twenty bucks," I said. "If I make the cheer team, you have to help me and Sofia film our contest video."

It was the perfect bet! I'd never actually join the cheer team, but if I could win the bet and get Dylan to film our video, we might have a chance of winning the contest.

Sofia's jaw dropped open. "You're really going to try out?"

"Um, yeah," I said. "If it means we might meet Tina Hart, I'd do pretty much anything."

Dylan hesitated. But he doesn't back down from bets, either. He finally said, "Deal. But while you're practicing your little cheerleading routine, I'm going to get some *great* video of you." He rubbed his hands together like an evil villain.

Reina laughed as she grabbed her backpack. "You'll be amazing, Joss. There are a couple of pre-tryout practices— tomorrow and Thursday. Six o'clock at the gym. See you then?"

As the door jingled behind her, my insides jangled. *Cheerleading?*

What had I just gotten myself into?

AT THE GYM

O n Wednesday night, while Mom and I waited in the driveway for Liam, I texted Sofia:

> If you don't hear from me in 2 hours, I was abducted by cheerleaders. Come rescue me!

I fidgeted with my Surf Sister bracelet, reminding myself why I was doing this. *To get Dylan's help with the video. To win the contest. To meet Tina Hart!*

Finally Liam hurried out the front door wearing his SoCal Board Shop shirt. We were dropping him off at work on the way to the gym. As he slid into the back-seat beside me, Mom caught my eye. "Are you nervous?" she asked, signing the word *nervous.* "And maybe a wee bit excited?"

I laughed. "*You* sound excited. You know I'm not going to be a cheerleader, right?"

She placed her hand on my shoulder. "Now, Joss. How do you know that if you haven't even tried it?"

"I'm a surfer, Mom," I said firmly. "I don't do pom-poms

or cheer on a bunch of boys. This is just to win the bet."

When Liam tapped my shoulder, I turned to face him.

He smiled. "Everyone knows you're a water girl, Joss. But Mom's right. You should keep an open mind. You might end up liking cheer."

I stared at him, wondering if aliens had taken control of his body. The *real* Liam knows I'm all about surfing, just like him. And just like Tina Hart.

Then it hit me—Liam had to say that stuff about cheer because his girlfriend is a cheerleader. But that didn't mean I had to listen.

When my phone vibrated, I read Sofia's text:

U-Rah-Rah, Joss!!! FB BB BB

"FB BB BB" stood for fist bump, butt bump, butt bump. I pictured Sofia doing the "U-Rah-Rah" part, too, flinging her arms around like she was shaking pom-poms. *Ha!* At least my Surf Sister could joke with me about cheer. So I was going to imagine that she and her pom-poms were with me tonight.

I'll go in there, memorize a few cheers, and do what I have to do to make the team and win the bet, I decided. *Then Sofia and I can get back to the Break, where we belong!*

After Mom checked me in at the front desk of Shine Athletics, she wished me luck, kissed the top of my head, and walked toward the waiting area.

Don't leave me! I wanted to holler. Instead, I took a deep breath and trudged toward the gym doors, my stomach fluttering. Why was I nervous? I mean, how hard could this be?

As I pushed open the doors to the gym, noise hit me like an ocean wave. Voices echoed off the walls and ceiling. Shoes thudded and squeaked against the mats. Music blared.

Now I had *plenty* of reasons to be nervous. How could I learn anything in here? I wouldn't be able to hear a word!

As I walked farther into the gym, I felt like a kook, a newbie at the Break trying to paddle out into a crowded lineup of local surfers. Except the ocean was never this crowded. And the gym was full of girls instead of trash-talking boys—girls who all seemed to be dressed alike.

A bunch of them wore matching turquoise tank tops and shorts. Matching white cheer shoes. Matching hair bows—*ginormous* hair bows.

I didn't see any pom-poms, but oh, those bows . . . *Guess I didn't get the memo,* I thought, running my fingers through my tangled hair. Not that I would have worn a bow anyway.

Dylan would have fallen over laughing at me.

On a distant mat, a group of older girls formed a pyramid. The girl on top stood on one leg, holding her other leg up by her ear. Suddenly, her teammates tossed her sky-high. She landed gracefully in their arms.

When she waved at me, I did a double take. That was Reina! *Whoa.* Sick trick!

As she jogged over to say hello, her ponytail bounced, but her zebra-striped bow stayed perfectly in place. She said something I couldn't catch—even though I really wanted to. "Sorry, I can't hear over the noise," I said. "Not without this."

I reached into my bag and pulled out the microphone I usually bring to school. It looks like a fat pen. When my teacher wears it around her neck, it sends her voice straight to a receiver on my hearing aid. "I'm supposed to give it to my coach," I explained. "Mom called her about it last night."

Reina's eyes lit up, and she nodded. Then she led me toward a woman holding a clipboard. Reina said something to the coach, who smiled.

The coach took the microphone from me and slipped it over her neck. "Nice to meet you, Joss. I'm Coach Kara," she said, her voice loud and clear in my hearing aid. "Ready to get started?" She waved me toward a group of girls.

Right away I recognized Brooklyn, a girl with tiny black braids pulled into a sparkly purple bow on top of her head.

She's in the other fourth-grade class at school. I also knew the girl with the sleek brown ponytail, at least her name. She's a fifth-grader named Mila. When she looked me up and down—from my loose hair, past my board shorts, down to my not-very-white sneakers—I fought the urge to stand a little taller.

Brooklyn bounded over and pointed to Coach Kara, asking me something I couldn't make out. She spoke so fast! But Coach Kara answered for me. "It's a microphone, Brooklyn. I'll wear it to help Joss hear me better."

I nodded. "It sends sound to my hearing aid," I explained to the other girls, who were suddenly listening.

Out of the corner of my eye, I caught Mila staring. "So can you hear us talking when we're *not* wearing micro-phones?" she asked loudly. *Really* loudly.

My insides bristled, but I held my voice steady. "Sometimes I can't hear over the noise in the gym. But that doesn't mean you have to talk louder." I stared hard at Mila when I said that. "If you speak normally and I can see your face, I can catch a lot of what you say."

Coach Kara smiled. "That's helpful, Joss. Thank you. Does anyone else have questions?"

One of the girls slowly raised her hand. "How did

you lose your hearing?" she asked.

I get that question a lot, so I had an answer ready. "I was born like this," I said. "But when I wear my hearing aid, it's not a big deal."

Brooklyn cocked her head. "Do you know sign language?" she asked.

"Yeah, I use it," I said. "Like when I don't have my hearing aid in down at the beach."

"Awesome," said Brooklyn. Her eyes widened, as if sign language were the coolest thing she'd ever heard of.

While we waited for practice to begin, I dug around in my shorts pocket for a hair tie. Mila crossed the mat toward me, looking like she had something to say. *Great.*

"You're that surfer girl, right?" she said. It didn't sound like a compliment.

"Yep, that's me." I finally managed to pull the hair tie out of my pocket—along with a handful of sand. *Oops.* I guess the last time I'd worn these shorts, I'd been at the Break.

As I brushed the sand off the mat with the toe of my sneaker, Mila wrinkled her nose, but I ignored her. I stared over the top of her turquoise polka-dot bow as I pulled my own hair into a low ponytail.

When the music stopped for one peaceful second, she asked, "So are you switching to cheer?"

"Switching?"

"Mila means are you switching from surfing to cheer," said Brooklyn, speaking more slowly now.

"No!" I said. "I'm just checking out cheerleading. It's sort of a bet with my brother. Long story."

"So you don't want to join cheer?" asked Mila, her hand on her hip.

When I shrugged, her face darkened, and Brooklyn's forehead wrinkled with confusion. As soon as the music started again, they both turned away. *Yikes.* Had I offended them?

That's okay, I told myself. *You're not here to make friends. You're here to win a bet, remember?*

Coach Kara led us in stretches and a jog around the gym, speaking into the microphone so I could hear her even when she was on the other side of the mat. Then she lined us up by a long skinny mat—a "tumbling track," I think she called it. As I waited for my turn, I patted my right ear, hoping my hearing aid would stay in place. The thudding bass of the music echoed through the gym, and I suddenly wished I were back at the Break, enjoying the silence and freedom of riding the waves without having to wear my hearing aid.

But after a pass or two down the track, I stopped thinking about my hearing aid—and the noise in the gym. I just went for it, cartwheeling after the girl in front of me. *Easy peasy,* I thought. So far, cheerleading was a cinch, just like I'd thought it would be.

Then Coach Kara asked one of the older girls from Reina's group to demonstrate front and back walkovers. I felt pretty proud when I pulled off a front walkover. I didn't need any help at all from Coach Kara, who was there to spot me. But when I tried a back walkover, I got *stuck* with my belly in the air.

While Coach Kara helped me kick my feet over my head, another girl *boinged* past doing back handsprings. *So maybe some of the girls in this gym are real athletes,* I had to admit. When the girl reached the end of the mat, I saw who it was.

Mila.

She waited for me at the end of the tumbling track. "I thought surfer girls were supposed to have super strong arms. How come yours are wobbling?" She smirked.

Well, that lit a flame inside me. There's nothing wobbly about the arms I use to paddle out to the lineup at the Break. I wanted to show Mila what this surfer girl could do.

I tried a back walkover again. But I still couldn't do it without Coach Kara spotting me, with one hand on my back and the other on my kicking leg.

"That's funny," said Brooklyn. "I can't do front walkovers, and you can't do back walkovers!"

Coach Kara chimed in as she stepped off the mat. "Most girls learn their back walkovers first. You're unusual, Joss," she said with a smile.

Was that a good thing or a bad thing? I couldn't tell. But I *was* unusual. I was a surfer girl in a gym full of cheer-leaders. *You don't have to be the best cheerleader in the room,* I reminded myself. *You just have to make the team.*

I was relieved when we finished tumbling—until we moved on to dance. Where was Sofia when I needed her? She wouldn't just learn the dance routine. She'd make up her own, and she'd make it fun, waving her imaginary pom-poms in the air.

When the music started up again, I couldn't hear Coach Kara counting off the steps to the dance moves. She was standing too close to a speaker, and the music blared in my ear. I didn't even know when to *start* dancing.

"Five-six-seven-eight! And one-two-three-four . . ." If I watched her lips, I could catch the count. But if I looked away for a second, I missed it. I tried to follow the other dancers' moves, but that left me a step behind everyone else!

Brooklyn shot me a worried look, as if she wanted to help but didn't know how.

Mila gave me a different kind of look. Her face spread into a smug smile, as if to say, *Go back to the Break, surfer girl.*

I couldn't let her get to me—not for a second. I *was* a surfer girl, and proud of it.

So when I make the team, I'll gladly go back to the Break, I thought, setting my jaw. *And I'll never look back.*

Dancing in the Sand

ⓒ CHAPTER 5 ⓢ

O n Saturday afternoon, as Dad, Sofia, and I walked toward the Huntington Beach Pier, we passed by the bronze statue of Duke Kahanamoku. Mom says the Hawaiian surfer is called "the father of surfing" because he brought surfing to Southern California more than a hundred years ago. As I passed by the statue, I looked up and whispered, "Thank you."

Sofia whirled around. "What?"

"Um, nothing. Just saying hi to Duke."

Sofia stared up at the chiseled bronze face. "What is he thinking?" she asked, studying Duke's expression.

I shrugged. "He's probably wishing he could get out on the water! I mean, can you blame him?"

I looked at the waves, which were perfect for surfing— and they almost always are. That's why Huntington Beach hosts an international surf competition every summer. Some of the best surfers in the world come right here to the pier to compete.

"Or maybe Duke is thinking about a milk shake," joked Dad.

I'd almost forgotten about the milk shakes waiting for us at the end of the pier. "Let's go!" I said, grabbing Sofia's arm.

We darted in and out of the stream of tourists walking along the pier. Some dangled fishing poles off the edge. Others lined up at souvenir shops or clustered around street performers, like the guy painted silver to look like the Tin Man. He stood as still as a statue until someone dropped a dollar in his cup. Then he moved his arms, all stiff-like, as if he really did need a can of oil.

By the time we'd made it to the red-roofed diner at the end of the pier, my stomach twisted. Was I hungry, or nervous about cheer? Tryouts were Monday, only two days from now. Just the thought sent a current of energy from my head to my toes.

"One Peanut-Butter-Cup Shake please," I told the woman at the counter, hoping I'd be able to eat it.

Sofia likes to mix milk shake flavors. She ordered a Black Cherry Mocha just as Dad caught up to us.

"Let's see," he said, rubbing his hands together. "What should I get?"

Sofia giggled because Dad always takes forever to choose—and then ends up getting something boring like vanilla. We left him at the counter and slid into a red leather booth, looking out the window toward Catalina Island.

Our milk shakes arrived, and Sofia took a long, slow sip.

Then she asked, "So, how's cheer going? Are you ready for tryouts?"

My ice cream stuck in my throat. "I still can't do the back walkover," I admitted. "I thought tumbling would be easy. But for some reason, I can't get it." *Maybe because of your wobbly arms*, I heard Mila say in my head.

"But you said the trampoline was pretty fun, right?"

I nodded. "The tramp was the best part of practice Thursday night. Some of those jumps felt like doing a front-side air—at least, how I think it would feel. But my dancing still stinks. I remember the moves, but it's hard to dance along with the other girls—we have to do the exact same moves at the exact same time! I can't make it up as I go along, the way we do when we surf, you know?"

Sofia gave me a sympathetic nod.

"When I told Coach Kara I couldn't always hear the count, she started holding up her fingers to cue me. That helped a ton. But I'm still about as graceful as Murph on a dance floor."

Sofia snorted—and then winced and grabbed the bridge of her nose.

"Are you okay?" I asked.

She squeezed her eyes shut. "Brain freeze. Ouch." When it passed, she glanced back up. "So let's download your music and work on your dance routine together, right here at the pier. I'll help you!"

"Here?" I started to sweat, even with the milk shake in my hands. I didn't want anyone—especially other surfers—to see me working on my cheer moves.

But I definitely needed help. And if my Surf Sister was offering it, I kind of had to take it. "Okay," I said with a sigh, "but don't say I didn't warn you about my dancing—it's not pretty."

She grinned. "I'm not worried."

Dad finished his vanilla milk shake, and we stepped back out onto the pier. As soon as the ocean breeze hit my face, I felt a flutter of hope. Why couldn't a surfer like me make the cheer team? I could. And I *would*. Especially if Sofia helped me with my dance moves.

"Hey, there's Liam and Reina!" said Dad, pointing over the rail at the volleyball courts below.

Liam plays pick-up games here on the weekends, and we sometimes throw down a beach towel and watch. But today, I didn't want to be anywhere near those courts. Liam said I should keep an open mind about cheer. But if he saw me dancing, he might think I was actually *liking* cheer—that I wasn't still a hundred percent surfer girl.

"Sofia and I are going farther down the beach to check the waves," I told Dad.

Once we were as far past the volleyball courts as we

could go without being out of Dad's sight, we spread out our towels. While Sofia propped up a cordless speaker in the sand, I scrolled through the songs on my phone and found the one I'd downloaded from the Team Shine website. I showed Sofia how to hold up her fingers to help me "hear" the count, the way Coach Kara had done at cheer practice.

Pretty soon, Coach Sofia was doing the same thing. "Five-six-seven-eight! And one-two-three-four . . ."

"Wait, start again," I said. My feet felt frozen in the sand. Plus, one of the volleyball games next to us had just ended. Was everyone watching me now? *Ugh.*

"Five-six-seven-eight! And one . . ."

On "one," I sprang into action, trying to remember the moves. *Step, crouch, arm cross. Clap, kick, turn. Neck roll, knee up, arms up—*

"Wait!" said Sofia, holding up her hand. "Try it like this." She did a neck roll, moving just her head and neck instead of her whole upper body like I did. Then she popped up her knee into the perfect pose. She made it look so easy!

I sighed, my shoulders slumping. "Maybe you should be the one trying out for cheer. You're a way better dancer than me."

Just then, I noticed Reina jogging up to us, her face shiny with sweat. "You're doing great, Joss," she said.

"Smile and try to look confident. As I like to say, *fake it till you feel it*! Want me to do it with you?"

I nodded, half mortified that she'd seen my lame moves and half relieved that there'd be someone doing them with me. "Thanks."

When Sofia started the music again, Reina and I did the moves side by side. *Fake it till you feel it*, I reminded myself. I pretended I was Reina, who could do this routine in her sleep. Or Sofia, who wasn't afraid to dance in front of strangers on the beach.

I got through almost all the moves and even smiled once or twice. I'd done my best, for sure. But as an image of Tina Hart flashed through my mind, I swallowed hard. If I ever wanted to meet my idol, I was going to have to do my best all over again at tryouts on Monday.

And I couldn't help wondering, *Will my best be good enough?*

TRYOUTS
CHAPTER 6

As I stepped into the gym on Monday, I felt like a flock of nervous seagulls had taken flight in my chest.

Brooklyn looked as if she were wearing one of those birds on her head. Her polka-dot bow was especially huge today. When she caught me staring, she said, "It's my good-luck bow. See?" She bent over to show me that the polka dots were actually tiny horseshoes.

"Cute." I meant it, sort of. If the bow weren't on the very top of her head, and if it were like seven times smaller, it would be pretty cute.

"Are you freaking out like me?" she asked, bouncing up and down on her toes.

I shook my head, even though those seagulls were threatening to fly right out of my mouth. *Never let them see you sweat.* That's what I tell myself at the Break, even when I'm trying my scariest tricks.

Brooklyn smoothed out her tank top and shrugged. "Well, *I'm* nervous." When she hurried off toward Mila, I was kind of sorry to see her go.

Then Coach Kara waved us over to the mat. "Some of you are asking if you can try out first, last, or somewhere in between," she said with a smile. "But you'll actually be trying out together, as a group."

Phew! So I wouldn't be performing alone, with everyone watching. When Brooklyn shot me a relieved smile, I gave her one right back.

As we took our places for the dance routine, I fixed my eyes on Coach Kara. She looked back at me, smiled warmly, and held up five fingers. *Five-six-seven-eight! And one . . .*

I barely had to think about the dance moves anymore. Thanks to Sofia and Reina, I'd practiced so much that my body just did them. And when I got to the neck roll, I pictured Sofia on the beach. *Fake it till you feel it*, I reminded myself.

I finished the routine out of breath and grinning. *Yes!* But it was too early to celebrate, because the tumbling part was next. That meant walkovers.

My knees wobbled at the thought. *Get it together, Joss.* I took a deep breath.

Reina caught my eye from the corner of the gym and gave me a thumbs-up. Seeing her made me feel like I was back at the beach on Saturday afternoon. So I pretended I was.

Trying out for cheer? Not me. I'm just a surfer girl paddling out to the lineup, ready to catch a wave.

That did it. My cartwheels were straight and strong.
I nailed my roundoffs, too, rebounding off the mat and catching some air after every one. But my back walkovers? *Ugh.*

"Let's start with a backbend," said Coach Kara into
the microphone around her neck.

I leaned backward until my hands were
planted on the floor. That was the easy
part.

"Now shift your shoulders over
your hands as you kick your leg off the
ground," she said, tapping my lead leg.

I tried. I kicked that leg as hard
as I could. But when it dropped back down, I did, too—and
landed flat on my back. I looked at Coach Kara upside
down. "I can't do back walkovers," I confessed. "I mean,
I can't do them *yet*," I added, remembering Liam's pep talk
about the frontside air.

She smiled as she helped me back up. "You're getting
there, Joss."

But my cheeks flushed hot as I got back in line.

I was relieved when it was time to move on to jumps.
These I could do! I raised my arms overhead in a high V
and pulled my body in tight for the tuck jump. I spread my
legs into a wide straddle for the toe touch and kept them

straight out in front for the pike jump. And I was pretty sure my front hurdler was higher than anyone else's.

Mila noticed, too. As we left the mat, she said, "Not bad."

Was that an actual compliment—from Mila?

"Not bad for a *surfer*, I mean," she added.

The warm fuzzy feeling in my chest turned into a prickly ball of irritation.

"Yeah, great jumps," said Brooklyn. "I wish mine were that good." She bounded off with a smile.

When Reina caught up to me, she pointed toward Brooklyn. "New friend?"

I shrugged. "She's nice." Then I lowered my voice. "But Mila? Not so much."

Reina leaned in. "I think Mila is just jealous of your jumps. They're so good!"

Pride flowed through me, washing away the bad feelings. "I think it's because my legs are strong from surfing."

Reina grinned. "Definitely! I knew a surfer like you would be good at cheer. But stick with cheer, and you might become an even better surfer."

Huh?

"We work on strength, flexibility, and balance here at the gym," explained Reina. "All of those would help your surfing. Plus, you could practice surf airs on the tramp during open gym!"

"Practice surf tricks at cheer?" I asked.

"Sure. I won't tell." She raised a finger to her lips, her brown eyes twinkling. "I think that's Tina Hart's secret. In her spare time, she goes undercover as a cheerleader." She cracked up at her own joke.

An image of Tina Hart wearing a cheer bow flashed through my mind, making me laugh, too. Still, I had to wonder: *If I keep doing cheer, could I learn to do a frontside air in time for the video contest?*

I tried picturing myself wearing that cheer bow—and landing a perfect frontside air. But the ginormous bow on my head started to grow. My legs wobbled under the weight of it. And pretty soon, I couldn't get off the ground at all.

That bow, and this cheerleading thing, just weren't me. Sure, I wanted to meet Tina Hart. But if I actually made the team, I'd have to draw the line at joining. Because I'm a surfer girl, one hundred percent.

Who also happens to love jumping on a trampoline.

The Big Decision
CHAPTER 7

R eady?" signed Mom. She was holding her tablet. It was Wednesday afternoon, and Mom, Sofia, and I were crowded on the couch, ready to see the results from cheer tryouts. I felt sick, but beside me, Sofia nearly sizzled with excitement.

As Mom opened the email from Coach Kara, I closed one eye and peeked through the other. The list of names was divided into teams based on age: tiny, mini, youth, junior, and senior. I skimmed the list—past Brooklyn's name and Mila's. When I didn't see mine, my stomach dropped.

"There!" Sofia pointed. Sure enough, there I was: *Joss Kendrick, Junior Level One.*

"You did it!" Mom said, squeezing my shoulders.

"Yes!" I gave Sofia such a fierce fist bump that we both shook our hands, laughing. "Now Dylan has to help with our video." My fingers flew as I texted him:

Made the team, bro. I win. You lose.
Get ready to film the Surf Sisters!

Then Mom tapped my shoulder. "So?" she said. "Are you going to join?"

Uh-oh. Where was Mom going with this? Sofia shot me a worried glance.

I cleared my throat. "No, Mom. I was trying out to win the bet, remember?"

She put her hand on my knee. "I get that. But remember that most of the girls who tried out really do want to join the team. If you don't, you need to email Coach Kara right away so she can give the spot to someone who wants it and can commit to it. Does that sound fair?"

I nodded. "I'll email her tonight." I knew Mom was right, but I wasn't looking forward to writing that email. Coach Kara had been pretty nice to me.

When my phone vibrated, I glanced down. Dylan had responded to my text with a video. I pressed PLAY and saw my goofball brother grabbing his throat and pretending to be dying. "You made cheer? Noooo! Say it isn't soooo!" He tumbled to the ground, right out of sight.

"Ha! That's what he gets for doubting me," I said.

"Right?" agreed Sofia. "Don't mess with Joss Kendrick." She squealed, bouncing on the couch. "Now you can finally quit cheer. I've missed my Surf Sister so much!"

Murph trotted into the room, wanting in on our celebration. Her tug-of-war toy dangled from her mouth. When

I gave it a yank, she tugged right back and growled, shaking her head from side to side.

Usually Murph wins tug-of-war. She's super strong. But today, I hung on tight. Because I wanted to win, too— the video contest, that is. And now, Sofia and I finally had a chance!

That night, I sat down at my desk and started a new email, using the address Mom had given me.

Dear Coach Kara,

Thank you for giving me the chance to try out for cheer. I've decided not to join the Junior Level One team, but it was a really good experience.

Joss Kendrick

I read the email and smiled. Mom would like that part about it being a "good experience." Satisfied, I hovered the cursor over the SEND button.

Murph nudged my leg with her nose.

"I know, girl," I said. "It's bedtime. I'm coming."

I read the email again. *Just send it already!* I told myself.

But for some reason, I didn't. Maybe it was because making the cheer team had been harder than I thought it would be. "Can't I just enjoy the win a little longer?" I said out loud.

Murph licked my leg.

"You're right," I told her. "I should sleep on it."

I clicked SAVE instead of SEND and then snapped my laptop shut.

I hoisted my board bag over my shoulder and hurried toward Sofia, who was crouched in the sand. She had created a bird out of shells, with plastic forks for legs.

"Wait, is that bird surfing?"

She grinned. "The surfboard is the perfect shape for a long word, if we can think of one."

"How about two words? *Super stoked!*" I said. "It feels so good to be surfing instead of practicing dance moves."

"Oh, come on," she said. "You rocked those moves. Let's see 'em!"

I pulled out a few, just to make her smile. Step, crouch, arm cross. Clap, kick, turn. Then I spotted Dylan behind the lifeguard tower, filming my every move.

"Dylan, stop!" I hollered.

He darted behind a beach umbrella and was gone.

It was Thursday afternoon at the Break, and life finally felt normal again. I was surfing instead of cheerleading. My brother was being a pain, but even that felt normal. I sank down onto my towel with relief.

Sofia set down her bag of shells. "So no more cheer?"

"No more cheer," I said, giving her a fist bump.

I mean, I hadn't sent that email to Coach Kara yet, but I would. *Tonight*, I promised myself. *Send that email already!*

But first? I was going to surf!

I gave my board a quick wax, moving the bar in circles until tiny bumps popped up—just to make sure my feet wouldn't slip while I was shredding today. Then I took out my hearing aid and tucked it into its case.

Beside me, Sofia smeared sunscreen on her face. "Ready?" she signed.

I grinned, like I do every time Sofia uses ASL. Only my Surf Sister would learn a few signs just for me. "Ready!" I signed back.

I grabbed my board and raced past Dylan. "Film me?" I called, flashing him a grin. "A bet's a bet."

He gave me a weak thumbs-up. Then I paddled out to the lineup.

Everything about the water felt right today. The waves

were peaky and peeling, the perfect shape for surfing.
I could feel their power and energy, pushing me back
toward shore. But I kept paddling. As I duck-dove under
an oncoming wave, my grip on my waxed board felt tight
and strong.

When I caught my first wave, I felt so alive, so free! No
more routines. No more steps to learn or counts to listen for.
Just me on the water, making it up as I went along.

I zigzagged up and down the face of the wave, until
I remembered that Dylan was filming. *Tina Hart might see
this video*, I realized. That was the shot in the arm I needed.
Time to do something.

When I reached the bottom of the wave, I pumped my
legs for speed. As I zoomed back up, I eyed the crest, ready
to do a dramatic top turn. I drove the nose of my board off
the lip of the wave—*way* off the wave. *Whoa!*

Before totally losing my board, I twisted my upper
body and flipped my board around—just in time. Relief
flooded my chest. Or maybe it was adrenaline. Or both!
But as I glided back down the wave, I grinned from ear to
ear. I'd practically done an air. *Yes!*

Had Dylan caught the trick? *He'd better have*, I thought as
I rode the wave out. I suddenly felt like I could do anything.

When I paddled back out to the lineup, Sofia gave me a
thumbs-up. I waited for her to catch a wave. And then Nico.

And when I spotted my perfect wave, I went for it.

This time, I didn't waste precious time carving back and forth. I got the speed I needed and aimed for the lip of the wave—the ramp that would take me airborne. *There!* I zoomed upward and got ready to jump.

Just like at cheer, I thought. I'm pulling off a tuck jump, like the ones Mila said "weren't bad for a surfer." It was time to show her what this surfer could do.

As I launched off the wave, I tucked my knees to my chest and reached down to grab my board, as if I were popping an ollie on a skateboard. I didn't think about it. I just *did* it.

Time slowed down—long enough for me to realize that I'd forgotten something important.

I'd forgotten that I still had to land!

But where?

At the last second, I panicked and let go. I tried to fall away from my board so I wouldn't smack into it. Then I tumbled into the wave like a rock in a washing machine.

But one thing softened my fall: the realization that I'd *almost* done a frontside air.

As I plunged deeper into the water, I smiled.

"Play it again!" said Sofia.

I tapped the arrow on my phone. There I was, launching off the wave with my board. Dylan had sent me the video, and I'm not going to lie—I felt a rush of pride watching it.

"Wow," said Sofia. "Nice wave, girl. I've never seen you catch that much air!"

I shrugged. "I never have—except maybe on the trampoline at cheer."

As I said the words out loud, I suddenly wondered . . . was Reina right about cheer practice making my surf tricks better? I mean, I'd only been to a few practices. But what would happen if I went to a few more?

"Was that the frontside air?" Sofia asked.

My cheeks flushed, this time with embarrassment. "It was supposed to be. I know you said that trick was too hard, and it probably is, but . . ."

She held up her hand to stop me. Then she pointed toward her beach art. Had she finished it while I was drying off? Sure enough, in the middle of her surfboard were three words: TRYING NEW THINGS.

"I'm starting to think that no trick is too tough for you," said Sofia, holding out her hand for a fist bump.

After dinner, I went to my bedroom for some QT—but I couldn't get Sofia's beach art out of my head.

Cheer was definitely "trying new things." And practicing surf tricks at cheer wasn't that crazy of an idea. I mean, I already practiced surf tricks on my skateboard. So why couldn't I practice them on a trampoline, too?

There were only so many perfect waves I could catch at the Break between now and the video contest deadline. But I could catch lots of air on a trampoline.

Maybe it was the rush of almost doing a frontside air today. Or maybe it was Sofia's vote of confidence in me. Or maybe it was my Tina Hart poster, reminding me that I could meet her and maybe even surf with her, if I could only land that frontside air in our video.

Somehow, I suddenly knew exactly what I needed to do. I flipped open my laptop, found my email to Coach Kara that I'd saved last night, and changed it—just a little.

Dear Coach Kara,

Thank you for giving me the chance to try out for cheer. I can't wait to join the Junior Level One team! It will be a really good experience.

Joss Kendrick

Then, before I could chicken out, I clicked SEND.

Bow On, Bracelet Off

I've decided to join the cheer team," I announced as Sofia and I walked into our classroom Friday morning.

She stared at me as if I'd sprouted a unicorn horn. "You *what*?" she asked—way too loudly.

Our friend Harper looked up from her desk.

"Shh!" I took Sofia by the elbow and led her to a corner of the room. "I'm just doing it to help us win the contest! Reina says I might be able to learn the frontside air if I keep practicing on the trampoline at cheer."

Sofia spun her Surf Sister bracelet around her wrist, but she said nothing.

So I kept talking. "You saw my frontside air last night. I didn't land it, but that was my very first try. Think how good it could get if I practice at the Break *and* on the trampoline. If I can land it in our video, we could win!"

Sofia shook her head. "I thought we [*mumble, mumble*] that the video wouldn't be about just one trick."

My chest tightened, like it does when Murph thinks she's a lapdog and sits on me. "It won't be about just one trick. But . . ." How could I make Sofia understand?

Then I remembered her beach art. "Your art will show Tina Hart that you're all about protecting sea animals—just like her—right? I want to prove that I can *surf* like her, too. If I can do a frontside air, the way she did at the Break when she was my age, she might pick our video to win. Then we could actually surf with Tina. Don't you want that?"

Sofia's gaze drifted. Was she daydreaming about surfing with Tina? Then her eyes flickered back. "How many nights a week do you practice cheer?"

"Two team practices. Plus . . . one night of tumbling." I added the last part quietly, hoping she wouldn't hear.

"*Three* nights? But when are we going to surf—and make our video?"

"Weekends," I said firmly. "Every weekend. I promise." Then I waited for Sofia to say something. And waited some more.

She finally answered. "Okay, but we're doing this together, right?"

"Yes. Together. Surf Sisters forever." I put out my fist.

She hesitated and then gave me a fist bump.

So my Surf Sister was on board with my master plan, at least sort of. Now I kept my fingers crossed that it would actually work.

Before cheer practice on Monday, I laid out my cheer gear: blue and black Team Shine leggings, a cropped top with a sheer tank to wear over it, and cheer sneakers.

"Cheer is a commitment," Mom had said before we'd gone shopping. "Not just of time, but also of money."

That meant I'd have to wait even longer to get a new surfboard. But that was okay—because if this whole cheer thing earned us first place in the video contest, I'd win a new board!

I quickly changed into my practice gear. Then I reached into the plastic bag and pulled out the super sparkly, purple, big-as-my-head bow. *Here goes nothing*, I thought as I gathered my hair into a ponytail. But instantly, the bow flopped sideways.

"Mom, help!" I called down the hall.

When she saw my emergency, she grabbed her tablet. "I think there were instructions on the Team Shine website about how to put that on. Yes, right here."

As we stood in front of the bathroom mirror, I read the first step out loud. "Pull the hair straight up from the ears into a ponytail." Mom started pulling. "Ouch, not so hard!"

"Sorry, sorry."

I showed her the next step, and pretty soon Mom had the purple bow wrapped tightly around my ponytail. It lay down flat on my head and didn't look half bad! So I read on. "Make sure the bow stands up straight on your head instead of flat like a helicopter."

Mom's eyes met mine in the mirror, and then we looked at my bow. Yep, I pretty much had a helicopter on my head. So we started over.

When Dylan pounded on the door, I groaned. I wasn't ready for him to see me with a cheer bow—or a helicopter—on my head. *Just get it over with,* I told myself. *Like ripping off a bandage.* I flung open the door.

The second Dylan saw me, he burst out laughing and toppled to the floor in his usual dramatic way. Then he stopped laughing. "Wait . . . are you actually joining cheer?"

I nodded, feeling the bow bob on my head. "But only to help with my surf tricks. Reina says jumping on the trampoline can help me learn the frontside air."

"Ha! I'll believe that when I see it," said Dylan. As he got to his feet, he shook his head. "So my surfer sister is turning into a cheerleader. What's this world coming to?"

"I'm not turning into anything," I argued. "Except a better surfer. You'll see."

But when I looked in the mirror, all I could see was my ginormous bow. I sure didn't look like a surfer. What would Tina Hart think of that bow? What would she think of *me* right now?

"Time to go," Mom signed before giving my bow one more tweak. "You ready?"

I took a deep breath and nodded. *Here goes nothing.*

As I followed Mom into Shine Athletics, I ducked, fearing the cheer bow on my head might not clear the door frame.

Mom turned and smiled. "I'm proud of you, sweetie, for trying something new."

"Thanks," I mumbled. But I wasn't just trying some-*thing* new. I felt as if I was pretending to be some*one* new— like I'd put on a Halloween costume and was acting out a part.

My cheer shoes suddenly felt tight. I missed my flip-flops. Plus, I felt like I had to stand perfectly straight so I wouldn't lose my bow, like when Sofia and I pretended we were models and balanced books on our heads.

As soon as I stepped into the gym, I caught Mila staring at me. *She probably doesn't recognize me in my cheer gear*, I decided. *I don't even recognize myself.*

At least I had my Surf Sister bracelet on. And anyway, it didn't matter what I looked like on the outside. *I'm still a hundred percent surfer girl on the inside*, I reminded myself.

Mila strode toward me. "I see you left your hair tie and your pocketful of dirt at the beach today. So you decided to join cheer?"

I rolled my eyes—just a little. "I made the team," I snapped. Obviously I'd made the team, or I wouldn't be here. But I wanted to remind Mila that I *deserved* to be here. This "dirty" surfer girl had earned her spot.

Coach Kara waved us over to the group, and we did a few stretches. Then we warmed up with laps around the gym. When Mila passed me, I sped up—even though it wasn't a race. Something about that girl made me want to win.

As soon as warm-ups ended, I realized something. I'd forgotten about the bow on my head! Was it still there? I reached up to check. Somehow, magically, it was. So maybe I didn't have to be so careful. Maybe I could still give my all to my jumps—and to mastering that frontside air.

When Coach Kara split us into two groups, my group got to start on the trampoline. *Yes!*

This is what it's all about, I thought when it was my turn.

Every jump felt like soaring over a wave at the Break, like I was flying high and reaching for the sky.

I started imagining myself actually surfing. I glanced sideways, as if looking for my landing on a wave below. I even reached down to grab the edge of my imaginary board.

"Was that a tuck jump, Joss?" Coach Kara's voice rang out in my ear as she spoke into the microphone. "Eyes straight ahead! Arms up in a high V!"

Oops.

"Your hurdler looked good, though," said Brooklyn as I hopped down off the trampoline. Leave it to her to say something nice, even after Coach had corrected me.

"Awesome tuck, surfer girl," joked Mila. Leave it to *her* to say something not so nice.

During tumbling, Mila kept flying by, showing off her handsprings. And when one of my walkovers wobbled, she was the first to notice. She was acting like Dylan at the Break, except here, I didn't have Sofia to back me up.

I twisted my Surf Sister bracelet around my wrist, and when Coach Kara came over to spot me, she saw it. "No jewelry at practice, Joss. Can you take that off, please?"

Take it off? I hadn't taken this bracelet off since the day Sofia gave it to me!

"It isn't jewelry," I explained, showing it to her. "It's

a homemade friendship bracelet."

"It's very pretty," she said. "But it could get caught on someone's finger and cause an injury. Please put it with your other things." She pointed toward the hooks where we hang our jackets and backpacks.

As I walked off the mat, my lip quivered. I *always* wore this bracelet! It was like having a piece of my Surf Sister with me wherever I went. And tonight at the gym, I really needed her.

Mila sidled up next to me. "*Real* cheerleaders know the rule about jewelry," she said.

"Well, I'm not a cheerleader," I snapped. "I'm a surfer who does cheer. There's a difference."

But if those words were true, why did I let Mila get to me so much? Why did I even care what that cheerleader thought?

Probably because the whole time I was telling her I was a surfer, I was taking my Surf Sister bracelet off. Now I had a bare wrist and a huge bow on my head. *Cheer bow on, surf bracelet off.*

What am I even doing here? I wondered. *I want to meet Tina Hart, but . . . is this worth it?* I had lots of questions, but I couldn't come up with any good answers.

DOG BEACH

CHAPTER 9

Sofia nudged my arm. "Look, Liam is taking Murph out again!"

I searched the waves for my bulldog. There she was! Liam hoisted Murph onto her boogie board, using the handle on her doggy life vest. Then he pushed her into deeper water and angled her board toward the beach.

As a wave lifted the board, Liam let go—and Murph barked with joy. She crouched low and stuck her rump in the air.

"Nice wave, Murph!" I called as she rode the wave in. Then I settled back onto my towel with a sigh. "I wish I were having that much fun out on the water."

Normally, I love Dog Beach, which is just up the coast from the pier. What's better than watching dogs play in the sand and romp through the water? But the waves here today were *way* too mushy to surf. I'd tried the frontside air three times, but I could barely pull off a decent snap.

Sofia caught my eye. "You don't think working on beach art is fun?" she asked.

"Well, yeah, of course it is," I said quickly. I wanted to

help Sofia with her art. But the truth was, I'd much rather be working on my surf tricks.

I broke a stick into pieces and used it to form the letter E in the word *friend*. Beside me, Sofia was outlining a ship made of seashells, with a broken plastic shovel for its sail. *Friend* plus *ship* equals *friendship*. Another genius idea from my Surf Sister.

As I finished my E, I saw her glance at me and grin.

"What?" I asked.

"I'm relieved you still want to surf," she said. "I thought you might have turned into a cheerleader after a week at the gym." She raised one eyebrow, the way only Sofia can.

I snorted. "No way. Never gonna happen."

She shrugged. "I was worried you might [*mumble, mumble*] in those matchy-matchy clothes, waving your pom-poms and screaming, 'Go, sports! Go, Dyl-an!'" She shook her arms in the air like a wild woman.

"Stop!" I hollered, grabbing at her arms until we both fell sideways, laughing.

"Hey!" she said. "Don't ruin our hard work." She straightened out a stick.

"Sofia, listen," I said. "All-star cheerleaders like the girls at Shine Athletics don't wave pom-poms. And they for sure don't cheer on boys—they do their own stunts and stuff. They're actually pretty good athletes." An image of Mila doing back handsprings flashed through my mind. "But I am never going to turn into a cheerleader, okay?"

"Phew." Sofia pretended to wipe sweat off her brow. "So have you been practicing your frontside air on the tramp?"

"A little bit," I said. I didn't tell Sofia that Coach Kara had caught me doing a surf trick instead of a cheer jump, or that Mila had been snarky about it. "But I've done a ton of stretching and leg exercises. I already feel more flexible and stronger." I flexed my thigh muscle and punched it with my fist.

Sofia laughed. "Awesome, muscle girl." She gave her sack of shells, stones, and sticks a quick shake. "Uh-oh. I'm getting low. We might need to do some beachcombing."

I checked out the beach, where a dachshund ran with a stick twice its size, and a Corgi played tag with the surf. "Yikes," I said, eyes wide. "I'm not sure Dog Beach is the best place to pick up things in the sand. You never know *what* you might find."

Sofia burst out laughing. "True. But it'll be fun—if you help me!"

As I started to get up, Murph suddenly bombarded me with a face lick.

"Gross! Too much love, Murph." When I pushed her away, she ran for her boogie board as if to say, *Take me out! Please, please, please!*

Liam jogged up behind her. "Sorry," he said, grabbing the harness on her doggy vest. "Why aren't you two surfing?"

"Because the waves are total mushburgers!" I cried. "I'm surprised Murph can even catch one."

He laughed. "Mushy waves are great for trying your frontside air! You probably can't land it yet, right? So why not practice at a break where you can wipe out in super soft waves?"

Huh. Good point. My big brother was full of them.

Liam pried the foam boogie board from Murph's mouth and then raced her toward the water. When Liam tossed the board into the shallow surf, Murph waded out after it.

Then I saw Dylan filming from shore. And I remembered: Dylan had agreed to help Sofia and me with our video, but he was also competing against us. And he was going to have Murph the Surf Dog in his video.

Argh. Who can compete against a surfing bulldog? Sofia and I were going to have to step up our game.

Sofia tugged on my hand. "Let's go," she said. "Beach treasures await!"

"Okay, but . . ." I glanced again at Dylan, who was getting more video footage by the second. "Is it okay if I go back out and try a few more airs instead?"

Her face fell. "You just said you'd help with my art!"

"I know, but Liam's right. This could be a good place

for me to practice my airs—or at least my wipeouts."
I cracked a smile, but Sofia didn't.

"We did all this work on the ..." she said, talking way too fast for me to catch every word. "If we don't ... it could get ruined!"

As if right on cue, the dachshund we'd seen earlier blew by. He paused just long enough to steal part of my F in *friend*. Then he tore off with the prized stick in his mouth.

Sofia let out an enormous sigh and sat back down. She mumbled something.

"What?"

"Go. Surf." Now she spoke a little *too* slowly. "It's fine." She signed the word *fine* and pursed her lips.

I could tell things weren't really fine—but I also didn't want to waste another second when I could be working on my frontside air! So I promised Sofia I'd be back soon. Then I took out my hearing aid, grabbed my board, and ran for the water.

I caught Dylan's attention as I jogged past. "Got me?" I asked, pointing toward his phone. If I actually landed a frontside air, I wanted to be sure Dylan filmed it.

He gave me a thumbs-up, but he didn't take his eyes— or his camera—off Murph.

It was easy to paddle through the soft, slow waves to the lineup. When I got there, I thought again about

Liam's advice. I tackled the first mushy wave as if it were
a trampoline. I might not be able to jump as high on water,
but I didn't have to worry about coming back down either.
I just aimed for the foamy white water when I fell. And boy,
did I fall—again and again.

I didn't land a frontside air, but I caught some serious
air on some pretty pathetic waves. And I was starting to get
the steps down now: Kick the tail of the board down. Tuck
your knees to your chest. Look for your landing. And then
prepare to wipe out—at least for now.

After about my seventh wipeout, I checked to see if
Dylan was filming. Nope, he was chasing Murph down the
beach. *Figures.*

I paddled to shore, ready to help Sofia again. But where
had she gone? I finally spotted her dark head bobbing along
the beach toward the pier, which meant she'd given up on
waiting for me and had gone beachcombing without me.

But she'd left behind a message: The "ship" in her *friendship* art was now tipped on its side, as if it was sinking.

Uh-oh.

I set down my board, put in my hearing aid, and
sprinted after her. "Sofia, wait!"

I know she heard me calling her name—because she
started walking faster. But she didn't turn around until
I was right beside her.

"Can I help?" I asked, leaning over to catch my breath. I pointed toward her bag of shells.

"I found enough on my own," she said, giving her bag a shake. But she wouldn't look me in the eye.

"I'm sorry," I said quickly. "I know I was supposed to help you."

She shrugged. "It's okay. I just . . ." She trailed off and set her gaze past the pier, toward the Break.

"Just what?"

She turned to face me. "I just miss you at the Break. With you at cheer all the time, it doesn't feel like we're doing this video *together*."

I spoke quickly. "We will—I mean, we are. C'mon, let's find more stuff for your art. More shells. More rocks. More sticks . . ." I desperately searched the sand around me, but all I found was a half-buried flip-flop. "Hey, could we do something with this?"

When I grabbed the flip-flop, the strap broke right off. And the corners of Sofia's mouth twitched, as if she wanted to laugh—but wouldn't.

"We'll surf all day tomorrow at the Break, you and me," I said. "Where no dogs can steal your sticks. I mean, *our* sticks."

With that, she finally smiled.

The Face-Plant

As I stood in line at the tumbling track Tuesday night, I counted again. Two and a half weeks till the video contest deadline. Sofia and I had surfed the Break on Sunday. I wasn't anywhere close to getting the frontside air down— but at least my Surf Sister and I had some fun together, and Dylan had filmed some decent clips of our easier tricks.

Now it was time to try landing my back walkover again, and I was feeling hopeful. Last night, I'd tried to visualize it during QT, like I do with surf tricks. I could almost *feel* my legs kicking over my head. So today, when Coach Kara came over to spot me, I shook my head. "Can I try one on my own?" I asked.

I leaned back into a bridge. I shifted my weight over my shoulders, feeling the strength in my arms. Then I pushed off the floor with my foot, kicking as hard as I could. For just a second, my other foot left the floor, too.

"Stick with it!" Coach Kara's voice rang out in my ear. "You can do this!"

I thought I could. I really did! But then gravity took over, and I collapsed to the floor with an *umph.*

Boing, boing, boing. Here came Mila, showing off her handsprings. I waited for her smug smile.

"Lock your elbows next time," she said instead.

Was she actually giving me a tip? "Um, thanks," I said. But I didn't need Mila to coach me. When Coach Kara said it was time for the trampoline, I jogged away, ready to show off a few jumps.

When Mila got in line behind me, I felt even more fired up. Maybe I couldn't do back walkovers or handsprings, but there was a lot I could do on the tramp. *Right now.*

I started with tuck jumps, the ones that remind me of launching into a frontside air. But why stop there? I ran through the toe touch, the pike, and the hurdler, too.

I saw Mila's face below. She was impressed—she couldn't hide it. That fueled my fire. *Time to fly!*

I should have stuck with cheer jumps—Coach Kara probably wouldn't approve of anything else. But I couldn't help it! My muscles were begging to do the frontside air.

So I did one more tuck jump, pulling myself into a tight little ball. I turned my head and shoulders, looking for my landing. Except . . . I wasn't on my surfboard. And I wasn't in the water. My feet hit the trampoline before I expected them to, and I fell forward into a face-plant. My forehead stung as it smacked against the stretchy canvas.

When I sat up, my cheer bow dangled sideways from

my ponytail. And in the quiet of the gym, I realized I'd lost
something else—my hearing aid!

I patted my empty ear and immediately panicked.
"Stop!" I shouted to a girl jogging past. "Don't move!"

When Coach Kara hurried over, I told her what had
happened. She helped me find part of my hearing aid on
the trampoline—the plastic part that goes behind my ear.
Then she had every other girl in the gym on her hands and
knees, searching the mat for my small, nearly see-through
ear mold—the part that goes inside my ear.

"I *have* to find it," I said to Coach. "I can't hear without it!"

She patted my arm and said something I couldn't
understand. I wished for the gazillionth time that my Surf
Sister were here, like she is at the Break when I have my
hearing aid out and need some backup.

Hot tears stung my eyes, but I wouldn't let them fall.
I dropped to my hands and knees, desperately searching
for that ear mold. Where was it?

When Mila squatted beside me, I looked up and
instantly regretted it. She said something that I'm pretty
sure was *not* an offer to help.

I pointed toward my ear. "I can't hear."

When she tried again, I held up my hand, trying to cut
her off.

But she kept talking. The girl couldn't take a hint! She

spoke louder and pointed toward the trampoline, and this time, I understood. "Nice tuck!" *Really?* She was trash-talking me at a time like this?

I hollered back at her. "It wasn't a tuck jump. It was a *surf* trick!" I must have really belted it out, because a couple of the girls near us whirled around. Coach Kara did, too.

I wished a sinkhole would open up so I could slide right through that mat and disappear. But then a curly-haired girl named Cassie crawled out from under the trampoline with something in her hand. *My ear mold.*

Relief flooded my chest, but as I reached for the ear mold, my cheeks burned. So much for showing Mila what I could do! I'd done a mortifying face-plant, lost the most important thing I own, and announced in front of my coach that I was more into surfing than cheer—all in about five minutes flat.

After practice, Coach Kara waved me over. *Uh-oh,* I thought. *Is she going to scold me for trying the frontside air?*

"Joss, I want to invite you to open gym this weekend," she said. "Brooklyn, you, too."

Brooklyn came to stand beside me, looking just as confused as I felt.

"We have open gym Sunday afternoons. Reina and

some of the other older girls will be here to help out. Joss, you could work on those back walkovers."

My stomach twisted.

"And Brooklyn," Coach continued, "you could work on your *front* walkovers. Maybe you could even give each other some pointers."

Brooklyn grinned at me. "Sounds fun," she said. "I'll ask my mom!"

I tried to smile back, but I couldn't muster one. Because Sunday was a *surf* day—and a Sofia day. How could I go to cheer instead, especially after I'd worked so hard to reassure Sofia that we'd work on our video on the weekends?

Then Reina jogged over, saying something I couldn't quite catch.

"What?" I stepped closer.

"You can get in extra time on the trampoline," she said. "To work on your surf tricks." She winked.

Was she teasing me now? No. One look in her eyes and I could tell she was trying to help me, maybe even with that frontside air.

"Surf tricks?" I asked, just to be sure.

She nodded. "Whatever you want to work on. That's why we call it 'open gym.' But you might want to wear a headband next time," she said, pointing toward my ear. "To keep everything in place."

She gave me a kind smile, but my cheeks burned all over again. "I will," I said. "Thanks."

"So you're coming to open gym on Sunday?" asked Brooklyn as Reina walked away.

I nodded. I had to go. If Reina still thought the trampoline could help with my frontside air, I needed all the time on the trampoline I could get.

At lunch on Wednesday, I watched Sofia take a big bite of grilled cheese sandwich. She stretched her head back, waiting for the string of cheese to break. Finally, she broke it with her fingers and popped it into her mouth.

I set down my fish taco and cleared my throat. "So my cheer coach says I need to do open gym on Sunday afternoon."

I was hoping Sofia would take a minute to swallow her food—that she'd take a breath instead of getting mad right away. But she totally tried to talk with her mouth full.

"What?" I leaned closer, watching her face. It's super tough to hear inside the noisy lunchroom. I always sit across from Sofia so I am facing her when she talks. But it's nearly impossible to understand a girl whose mouth is full of cheese.

She held up a finger and then swallowed. "Wait, does that mean you're not surfing on Sunday?" Her eyebrows pinched together.

I shrugged. "Not in the afternoon. But I'll get to work on the frontside air on the trampoline for like *two* hours."

Sofia didn't look impressed. "So now you're doing cheer on Sundays, too? Four days a week? You know you only have like [*scrape, clatter, clatter, scrape*]." As the boy across from us pulled his chair across the floor, Sofia watched him go. Was she waiting for the noise to stop so I could hear her? Or was she too frustrated to look at me?

"What?" I asked. I leaned sideways to see her face.

She faced me. "I said you only have like a week and a half to learn the frontside air!"

I shook my head. "I have two and a half weeks!"

"No," she said firmly, "because we have to leave time for editing the video, too."

Yikes. Somehow a week and a half seemed a whole lot shorter than two.

"What if you don't learn the trick in time?" she asked. "Four days a week is a lot of time for [*crinkle, crinkle, crinkle*]." The girl next to me opened a bag of chips.

"For *what*?"

"For one trick! Can't you just quit cheer and have Dylan film the tricks you know you can do? You're going to quit after the contest anyway, right?"

Her question hung in the air.

"Yeah, I mean . . . right." The truth was, I hadn't thought that far ahead about cheer. But I for sure wasn't ready to give up on the frontside air.

So I tried again. "You know how you worked so hard on your art at Dog Beach," I said, "and you wanted to finish it before some kid ran over it—or a dachshund stole your letters?"

She didn't smile.

"Well, I've been working hard on my frontside air, too. If I quit trying now, all that work will have been a big waste. I won't have any awesome tricks to put in the video, so we might never get to meet Tina Hart. I'm just trying to help us win!"

Sofia shrugged. "I know. But cheer is taking all of your time. If you'd drop the dumb frontside air, you could quit cheer and come back to the Break, where you belong. I miss you!"

My frustration melted like the cheese in her sandwich. "I miss you, too, Sof."

We both stared at the table for a second, fiddling with our food. How could I make things better?

The words came out of my mouth before I'd even thought them through. "I'll make you a deal," I said quickly.

"If I don't nail the frontside air by a week from Saturday, I'll quit cheer, and we can spend the whole next week making our video as good as it can be."

Something shifted in her eyes, and she slowly held out her fist. "Deal."

With a fist bump, the deal was sealed. But as I finished my lunch, I did the math in my head. In the next week and a half, there were four cheer practices, two hours of open gym, and a couple of weekend days to surf the Break. Would it be enough time to learn the frontside air?

And if it wasn't, *could* I quit cheer? Would Mom even let me after all that talk about commitment? *Ack!*

I felt like a surfer without a plan, like I'd gone up for a frontside air without having a clue how to land it. And I only had a week and a half to figure it out.

THE GOOFY-FOOTED CHEERLEADER

I like it!" Brooklyn pointed to the yellow headband that held my hearing aid in place.

"I hope it works," I said. "If I lose my hearing aid again, I'll probably die of embarrassment."

It was Sunday afternoon at open gym. With fewer girls here, it was much quieter. Brooklyn and I could actually have a conversation! And she was suddenly *very* chatty.

"Don't be embarrassed," she said. "I lost my retainer once. I accidentally threw it away in the trash during a field trip, and the whole class had to dig through gross food wrappers until we found it." She wrinkled her nose.

Then she started talking faster. I only caught a couple of the gory details: Her retainer was covered in barbecue sauce, and kids started calling her "Barbecue Brooklyn." When she finished the story, my stomach hurt from laughing.

"Thanks," I said. "I feel better."

Someone tugged on my ponytail. Reina!

"I'm so glad you two came," she said. "Now I can help you with those walkovers." She pulled out her phone.

"Let's film your skills, okay? It's a great way to see what you're doing wrong—and right."

Reina spotted my back walkover while Brooklyn filmed us. Then we watched the clips together.

I really look like a cheerleader, I thought with a start, from the bow on my head to the way I arched my back and pointed my toe. And I looked super strong, too, even my arms—no matter what Mila had said. So why couldn't I kick my leg over? I glanced up at Reina.

"Are you right-handed?" she asked.

I nodded. "But I'm goofy-footed."

"Huh?" Brooklyn laughed.

"On a surfboard or skateboard," I explained. "Like when I skate, I put my right foot forward and push with my left."

Reina tapped my arm. "So maybe you're a goofy-footed cheerleader, too," she said thoughtfully. "Try starting the walkover with your right foot forward. As you lean back, kick off with your left."

I was willing to try anything. So I did the trick again, following Reina's tip.

She stood beside me, ready to spot. But I never felt her hands on my back. As I kicked off with my left foot, my legs floated right over my head. "I did it!"

Brooklyn grabbed my hands, and we spun around the mat. Reina laughed as she filmed our victory dance. You'd think I had just nailed the frontside air or something!

It turned out that Reina had all kinds of great tips. When Brooklyn started her front walkover with her shoulders hunched up, Reina tapped the top of her head and said something.

"What was that?" I asked.

"I told her to use her bow," said Reina. "Imagine your bow is lifting your head and neck upward while your shoulders stay down."

Brooklyn must have tried it, because I saw her chin lift a little higher.

"It works with jumps, too," Reina told me. "Imagine your bow pulling you up."

I wasn't so sure about that, but after we'd filmed some of Brooklyn's front walkovers, I asked Reina if I could hit the trampoline. I started with a few cheer jumps. Then I tried the frontside air, running through the steps in my mind: *Kick the tail of your board down. Tuck your knees. Look for your landing.*

I imagined my bow pulling me higher as I tucked. And I practiced my timing, too—looking for my landing right away, and snapping my legs back down. I did not need another face-plant in my future.

When I caught Brooklyn watching, I laughed. "I look pretty weird, right?"

She shook her head and gave me a thumbs-up, which

was almost like having Sofia cheer me on at the Break. Then I saw that Reina had filmed my jumps. "Got it!" she said, tapping her phone. "I'll send these to you."

When I finally climbed down off the trampoline, I was smiling from ear to ear. I'd gotten tons of practice on the tramp. Plus, with Reina's and Brooklyn's help, I'd done a back walkover. Finally! So maybe, just maybe, the frontside air was possible, too.

I couldn't wait to try it again in the water. *Will I have time to hit the Break tonight?* I wondered.

While I waited for Liam to pick me up, my phone vibrated with messages from Reina. I scrolled through the clips she'd sent. My tuck jump looked awesome. If I blurred my eyes and imagined my surfboard beneath my feet, I could almost see myself doing a frontside air.

I texted the best clip to Sofia—the one of me soaring high with Brooklyn cheering me on—and added a quick message:

> Got lots of trampoline time today! Gonna TRY to hit the Break tonight and land the frontside air—for real!!! Can you come?

When I glanced up, I saw Liam in his aqua-blue surf bus pulling up in front of the gym. *Yes!* I grabbed my things and rushed out the door.

Liam was still in his board shorts, his hair wet from surfing and his calves caked with sand. He must have come straight from the Break.

I sort of wished Mila were here to see him. *Surfers are grungy*, she'd probably think, wrinkling her nose. And sometimes we are. But Liam is also about the coolest guy I know—grunge and all. Even Mila couldn't argue with that.

As I slid into the front seat, I skipped the hello and blurted, "Can I go back to the Break with you?" I pulled Sofia's trick and gave Liam my best puppy dog eyes.

He grinned. "Don't you have homework?"

"Already finished it," I said proudly. "Except this one surf trick that I've got to practice for a 'test' next weekend."

He laughed. "All right. Let's head to the Break and I'll help you with your 'homework.'"

Woohoo!

I texted Sofia again:

Where are you? Liam and I are taking the Surfmobile to the Break. Meet me there!

Even after I'd stopped at home to change clothes, I still hadn't heard back from Sofia. So when Liam and I got to the Break, I was surprised to see her leaning against the bike rack outside her mom's shop.

"Where've you been?" I asked her. "Did you get my texts?"

She nodded. "I can't surf though," she said. "I'm doing homework while Mom sets up a display." Then her gaze fell to my wrist—and stayed there.

I looked down and realized I'd forgotten to put my Surf Sister bracelet back on. "Oops! I had to take it off for cheer," I explained. "It's a safety thing."

Her face darkened. Was she still mad about me doing cheer on a Surf Sunday?

I wished she'd been with me at the gym. Then she would have seen that time on the tramp was helping my frontside air. But, wait . . . she *had* seen. I'd sent her a video of one of my jumps. "Did you watch the video?" I asked her. "The one I texted you?"

Her eyes flashed. "You mean the one where that cheer-leader was cheering you on? 'U-Rah-Rah! Go, Joss!'" She shook her hands as if they held teeny-tiny pom-poms. But her jaw tightened, and I could tell she was upset.

"You *know* that cheerleader," I said. "That's Brooklyn

from school. And yeah, she was cheering me on. Because she's super nice."

Sofia shrugged. "I just never knew that you two were BFFs. Or that you were having such a blast at cheer."

Was she jealous or something?

"I'm not having a blast. I mean . . . I don't know. I'm only doing cheer to get better at my frontside air, Sofia. And I am getting better. If you'd surf with me tonight, you'd see that!"

She shook her head. "Sorry, I can't." She gave the most pathetic wave and then turned away and went inside her mom's shop.

I stared after her until my own hurt reflection gazed back at me from the glass door.

When Liam shot me a questioning look, I shrugged. *What's going on with me and Sofia? I don't even know anymore.* But I didn't feel like talking about it. All I wanted to do was surf.

Liam and I walked to the beach in silence. As I laid out my towel, he tapped my arm. "Frontside air? You and me?"

I blew out my breath. "Yeah. If I can do it by next Saturday, I get to—" *Whoa.* I'd almost said, "I get to stay in cheer."

Get to? That made it sound like I was loving cheer! Liam had told me to keep an open mind, but I didn't want him to think I'd switched teams, that I wasn't all in with surfing anymore. "I get to ... hopefully film the trick for the video," I said instead.

Liam grinned. "All right, then. Let's do it."

As I stepped into the waves, the cool water washed away my frustration with Sofia. Liam was here to help. I'd had a great day on the trampoline. And I *was* getting better at the frontside air—I was sure of it.

Even if my Surf Sister wasn't here to see it.

Stopped Motion

*B*efore I went to bed that night, I took out my hearing aid. Instantly, the sounds drifting through my doorway faded away—the grunts from Dylan's video game and the dramatic music from Dad's action movie. I climbed into bed, ready for some QT.

First, I thought about the frontside air I had *almost* pulled off tonight at the Break with Liam. My cheer jumps were helping my timing, for sure. And Liam taught me to stay low when it was time to land the trick. I'd nearly landed it!

But when I finally closed my eyes for QT, I didn't think about surfing. I thought about cheer.

If I can do the frontside air, I get to stay in cheer, I'd almost told Liam. But why? Did I want to stay in cheer? And if I couldn't land the frontside air by next weekend, would Mom even *let* me quit?

I flinched when a hand touched my shoulder. It was Mom—as if she'd stepped right out of my thoughts and into my room. "Sorry!" she signed, and leaned over to kiss me good night.

I almost asked the question out loud: *Can I quit cheer? Would you let me?*

But I didn't ask.

Why not? I wondered.

I mean, if Mom said I couldn't quit, I could forget this whole deal with Sofia—Mom would back me up on it!

But then again . . . what if Mom said I *could* quit cheer? Then I'd have to admit that I maybe, sort of didn't want to.

As Mom left the room, I scolded myself. "You're a surfer—not a cheerleader," I whispered into the darkness. "You can't be both."

Or . . . can you? asked a pesky little voice in my head.

Tina Hart stared at me from the wall. *Be all in. 100%.* But as my eyes drifted shut, those words began to blur.

Monday at school, Sofia was chilly—like the beach on a January night. She invited Harper to hang out with us at recess, which meant that we couldn't really talk. And later, when I walked into the cafeteria late, Harper was sitting in *my* spot.

I set my tray down next to Sofia. If I couldn't see her face, I had to at least sit with my hearing ear toward her. She still wasn't saying much to me, though.

Harper spoke first. "I saw the [*mumble, mumble*] video," she said. "Sofia showed me. It's awesome!"

"What video?" I asked, training my eyes on Harper's lips. Had Sofia shown her the video of me at cheer?

"The stop-motion video!" Harper explained.

I had no idea what she was talking about until Sofia pulled out her phone and hit PLAY. Suddenly, her beach art came to life—all on its own. Shells began dotting the sand, forming the outline of a ship. The word FRIEND spelled itself, letter by letter, with sticks—as if by magic.

I sucked in my breath. "Sofia," I said. "Why didn't you show me this?" I craned my neck so I could see her face as she spoke.

She shrugged. "I made it that day at Dog Beach. You were so into practicing your surfing tricks, I didn't think you'd be interested."

Her words felt like a punch to the gut. But what could I say? I hadn't helped her much that day. "It's cool," I finally said. "I mean *really* cool."

She smiled, but then her gaze fell to my wrist. "Where's your bracelet?"

Oh no.

"I forgot to put it on," I said quickly.

Her face went dark again. "Maybe you should . . ." She turned away before I could hear the end of the sentence.

"What?" I asked.

Harper waved at me. "She said maybe you should just leave it off."

Thanks, Harper. Very helpful.

"Why would I leave it off?" I asked, looking directly at Sofia.

Her face hardened as she turned to face me. "Because you're not really a surfer girl anymore."

My stomach twisted. How could she say that? I was so much a surfer that I was doing a whole other sport just to get better at surfing! I wanted to say that to Sofia, but my throat felt too tight.

We stared at each other as the buzz of voices grew around us, like a swarm of angry bees.

Then Sofia pushed back her chair, slid her tray off the table, and headed out of the cafeteria.

You're not really a surfer girl anymore.

Sofia's words followed me all the way to cheer practice.

I was tired of defending myself—against Sofia for not wearing my Surf Sister bracelet, and against Mila, who still thought a surfer girl like me didn't belong in a cheer gym.

So where *did* I belong? *Anywhere?*

As I took my last turn on the tumbling track, I tried to shake off Sofia's words the way Murph shakes off salt water at the beach. I pulled off another back walkover. I was rocking them now. I leaned backward and kicked my left leg—strong from being a goofy-footed surfer—off the mat to bring me upright again.

Brooklyn met me at the end of the mat. "You've gotten so good!" she said.

Mila noticed, too. "Look who *finally* got her back walkover! The surfer girl who does cheer!"

Those were the same words I'd said to her a couple of weeks ago. So why did they bother me now? Maybe it was the look on Mila's face, or the way she stood there with her hand on her hip.

"Give it up, Mila," I snapped. I turned on my heel and headed for the trampoline.

But she followed me. I felt her eyes staring at the back of my head as I waited for my turn. When she tapped my shoulder, I spun around—ready for battle.

Brooklyn appeared from out of nowhere and squeezed between us. "Your turn!" she said, pushing me toward the tramp. She stayed back in line to deal with Mila.

Wow, I thought. *Talk about taking one for the team.*

Sofia had teased me about having a cheerleader

cheering me on at open gym. But what was so bad about that? Brooklyn had my back right now way more than Sofia did.

As I warmed up with a few jumps, I thought about my promise to Sofia—that if I couldn't do the frontside air by Saturday, then I'd quit cheer. But now, the thought made me queasy, and it wasn't just because I was bouncing on the tramp.

Right now, cheer was about the only thing going well. I'd finally gotten my back walkover. Brooklyn and I were becoming friends. And I was loving time on the tramp.

I didn't want to quit cheer. Not yet.

So I kept jumping.

Toe touch. Pike. Hurdler.

Then I tucked my knees to my chest, imagining the frontside air. I gave it everything I had, hoping that by the time I got to the Break on Saturday, it would be enough.

Pummeled

As soon as I woke up on Saturday, I checked the surf report online. Perfect conditions: Medium-sized waves. Southwest wind. Clear skies. *No excuses.*

I pulled on a swimsuit and shorts and then raced into the bathroom to put my hair in a bow. My hand froze mid-air. What was I doing?

I wished I *could* wear the bow—to pull me sky-high as I launched into that frontside air. But I sighed and reached for a hair tie instead. I would just have to imagine the bow on my head. And Reina's hand on my back. And Brooklyn's cheers.

At the last moment, I grabbed my Surf Sister bracelet. "Today, you're a surfer girl," I told my reflection in the mirror. "One hundred percent. No matter what anyone says."

As I waxed my board, I scanned the beach one more time. Where was Sofia?

Dylan was wound up like an action toy. "Are we doing

this?" he asked, waving his phone in the air. "Do you need a drumroll? A cheering section?" He scooped up a handful of kelp that had washed ashore and shook it like a pom-pom. "Go, Joss! Woo-hoo!"

"Gross!" I swatted his arm. "Stop!"

He tossed the kelp over his shoulder, nearly hitting a woman walking behind him. "So are you ready or what?"

I took a deep breath and blew it back out. "I think so."

As I did a quick side stretch, I spotted Sofia standing by the lifeguard tower, as if that was as close as she was willing to get. Did she even want me to land the frontside air? Or did she want me to blow it—so I'd quit cheer altogether?

Either way, this is it, I realized. *My last chance at the frontside air.* I quickly took out my hearing aid. Then I grabbed my board and hit the waves at a sprint.

As I paddled out toward the lineup, I did a duck dive under a wave. And then another. And almost too soon, I was sitting in the lineup. Nico was there, plus a couple of Dylan's other friends. When the waves started rolling in, I sat back, waiting my turn.

I was surprised when Nico offered me his wave. I shook my head, but he kept insisting, until the wave passed both of us. Then it dawned on me. Dylan must have told Nico he was filming me—and maybe those other guys, too. They were waiting for me to do the frontside air!

I didn't know whether to thank Dylan or chew him out. Having first pick at the waves made me feel like a celebrity, like Tina Hart. But it also made me want to swim back to shore and hide under my beach towel.

When the next wave came, I took it. What choice did I have? As soon as I was on my feet, my adrenaline kicked in. I zoomed down the face of that wave so fast that I nearly lost my footing. But I didn't. I turned and flew back up.

You have been practicing for weeks, I told myself. *You've got this!*

When the right moment came, I launched off the lip of the wave. I mean, I *flew*. My legs felt so strong! I soared sky-high, imagining my cheer bow pulling me up. I had plenty of time to scope out my landing, to snap my legs back down.

But something went wrong.

My board shifted, tossing me into the white water. I spread my arms and legs like a starfish so that I wouldn't plunge too deep. And as soon as I surfaced, I tried to get my mind right again.

Don't quit. You caught so much air! You can do this!

As I climbed back onto my board, I glanced back at the beach. Was everyone still watching? Um, yeah. They weren't only watching—some of them were clapping. For *me*. Now I really did feel like Tina Hart. If there was ever a day when I could land the frontside air, this was it!

I set myself up to catch another wave, clenching my jaw with determination.

When the wave came, I popped up and carved a few lines before setting up for the trick. Then I went for it, my heart racing. *Give it everything you've got,* I told myself. *One hundred percent!*

As I launched off the wave, energy flowed through every inch of my body. I felt stronger than ever.

I wouldn't fall this time. I was going to stick the landing. I was!

But gravity took hold too soon.

No!

As I fell forward, I overshot the white water and headed straight for the flats. I slapped against the water, barely missing my board, and tumbled into the churning wave.

I plunged so deep that I could feel the pressure of the wave above holding me down. I needed to breathe. Or cry. Or scream. But I couldn't!

My leash tugged at my ankle, as if my board were trying to help me—to pull me back to the surface. But it wasn't strong enough.

Don't panic, I reminded myself. *Ride it out.*

I knew the wave would release me.

And it finally did.

I came up coughing and sputtering—but not crying.

I wouldn't let Dylan see me cry.

Still...I wasn't ready to take another wave. I needed a break to get myself together. So I headed toward shore.

No one was clapping for me now—at least not until I stepped out of the waves and they saw I was all right. Then Dylan waved to get my attention. He wobbled his knees as if reenacting my fall.

Really? In front of all these people? After I'd just gotten pummeled by a killer wave? Tears burned in my eyes again—angry tears.

More surfers had gathered on the beach now, but where was Sofia? There, behind Dylan. And she was...*smirking*. Like she thought Dylan's teasing was hilarious. Like she was *happy* that I'd bombed the frontside air!

I might as well have stepped on a stingray. But instead of being flooded with venom, I was suddenly filled with rage. Red-hot rage.

When Sofia headed my way, I ignored her. But she wasn't coming over to talk. Instead, she bent over to write something in the sand.

I watched her scrawl the words, letter by letter. And when I read them, my blood boiled.

TIME TO QUIT CHEER

"No!" I said through gritted teeth. "I can do the frontside air. And I'm *not* quitting cheer." I didn't know I'd actually made that decision until the words flew out of my mouth.

I spun around and raced back into the waves. I could do the frontside air—I knew I could. As angry as I felt right now, I could blast off into the stratosphere.

I paddled straight toward the lineup. The guys were still out there, watching and waiting. Were they laughing, too?

It didn't matter. I was done getting told what I could and couldn't do. Done trying to prove myself to the boys here at the Break, and even to Sofia.

I know what I can do. And no one is going to stand in my way.

I took the first wave that came along, spinning my board and paddling furiously to catch up with the wave. I turned my back on the ocean, and on all the surfers out there who thought I wasn't good enough.

I popped to my feet so fast that they barely touched my board.

And that's when I saw a surfer barreling toward me. *Nico.*

Where had he come from? I hadn't seen him. I hadn't even bothered to look!

Just before we collided, I dove off my board.

But it was too late.

The Snake

When I came to the surface, I searched for Nico. I wasn't hurt—I'd dove off my board just in time. But Nico had hit my board *hard*.

There he was, about ten yards away, doing something I've never seen brave Nico do. He held a hand in the air, the sign that he needed help. *Oh, no!* Was he hurt? Had he lost his board?

I paddled toward him, but another surfer got there first and offered Nico his board. As Nico threw his leg over the top, I saw the bloody gash on his ankle. It was a fin chop, from colliding with the sharp fin on a surfboard. *My* surfboard.

My heart sank to the bottom of the ocean as I followed them toward shore.

A lifeguard helped Nico sit down on a towel. I hurried toward him, not even stopping to put my hearing aid in. "Nico, I'm sorry!" I cried. "I didn't see you."

He gave me a lopsided grin and cracked some joke that I couldn't understand. But his face was pale and he winced when the lifeguard began cleaning his wound. Then Dylan stepped in front of Nico and said something to me.

"What?" I pointed toward my ear to remind him I didn't have my hearing aid in.

He didn't repeat the word. He signed it, hooking his pointer and middle fingers into the shape of fangs, and slithering his hand forward.

Snake.

My heart went cold. It was the worst insult a surfer can get—the word for someone who steals someone else's wave on purpose.

"I didn't mean to drop in on his wave!" I said again. "I just didn't see him!"

But Dylan didn't want to hear it. He stood before Nico like a shield while the lifeguard bandaged Nico's ankle.

I trudged back to my towel, my head hanging low. By the time I had dried off and put my hearing aid back in, Dylan was helping Nico across the sand toward the board shop.

"Dylan!" I called. "Wait up!"

He turned to face me. "You and Sofia are on your own with the video," he said. "You can finish filming by yourselves."

The words stung like sand hitting my face during

a windstorm. Then I noticed Sofia standing by the bike rack. Had she heard Dylan, too?

She must have. Storm clouds rolled across her face. "So now you're refusing to quit cheer *and* Dylan won't film our video?" she asked.

I bit my lip. I couldn't talk about cheer with Sofia right now—I was too angry. So I tried to focus on the video instead. "We can still finish the video," I told her. "Maybe we don't need Dylan—we can do our own thing. I mean, our video doesn't have to be perfect."

She snorted. "So *now* the video doesn't have to be perfect? Because you can't get the frontside air? Well, what about my art?" She threw up her hands. "You know what, Joss? You're already doing your own thing. You stopped caring about my thing a long time ago." She spun around and started walking away.

"Sofia," I called. "Stop!"

She faced me again and squared her shoulders. "You're not my Surf Sister anymore," she snapped. "You're not a surfer at all—you've pretty much turned into a *cheerleader*." She practically spit the word.

"So what if I am?" I shot back. "At least my cheer team-mates support me. Unlike you. You gave up on me doing the frontside air. What kind of a Surf Sister is that?"

She stepped toward me. "What kind of Surf Sister

insists on doing some show-offy trick?"

Show-offy? She thought I was trying to show off with the frontside air?

"The video was supposed to be about what we love most about the Break," she said. "Not about what you love best about yourself."

Something exploded in my chest. "Maybe you're just jealous because my surf tricks were actually getting better because of cheer!" I shouted.

Sofia held up her hand like she didn't want to hear another word. Her eyes had never looked so black. "We're not Surf Sisters," she said. "And we're not entering the video contest together. I'm done."

As she strode back toward the board shop, I stared after her. Bicycles streamed along the path between us. There were swimmers and surfers everywhere.

But I'd never in my whole life felt so alone.

Sunday morning brought June Gloom.

Usually, I hate the gray mist that rolls in from the water—the clouds that hang overhead all morning. But today, I welcomed the gray. Why waste sunshine when I was feeling so stormy inside?

I checked my phone, as if Sofia would miraculously text an apology. How could she bail on me a week before our video was due? And how could Dylan accuse me of being a snake? Dylan, who steals waves from me at the Break all the time. If anyone was a snake, it was him!

I don't need them, I decided. *Any of them.* Except I kind of did. Because the video contest deadline was coming up, and I didn't have any good clips. Not a single one.

I scrolled through the photos and videos on my phone, swiping past the ones of me and Sofia, because those ones hurt. But as I watched the clips of me and Brooklyn at cheer, I had to admit that Sofia was right about one thing.

I'm not a hundred percent surfer girl anymore. I'm a cheerleader, too.

Was that so bad? Yes, we wore matchy-matchy clothes, but that made us feel like a team! And yes, I had a huge bow on my head, but that bow gave me confidence. It helped me stand taller and jump higher. And yes, we cheered for each other at the gym—like Sofia and I *used* to do.

I glanced up at my Tina Hart poster on the wall. *Be all in. 100%.* How can a surfer who is also a cheerleader win a video contest that Tina Hart is judging?

I probably can't, I admitted. *So I'm not going to meet Tina Hart. All of my hard work was for nothing!*

I started to peel the poster off the wall, but then

I stopped. Even if I wasn't a hundred percent surfer girl, Tina Hart was still my idol.

And Sofia is still my best friend, I thought sadly. *Even if she isn't speaking to me.*

I checked my phone again and then set it on my dresser, facedown.

Monday night, I found Dad sanding up a storm in the garage. He was working on a ginormous longboard stretched across two sawhorses. I could tell the board was super old. The only place I'd seen a bigger surfboard was at the surf museum near the pier.

"It's going to be a picnic table," he said. "What do you think?"

I cocked my head. I couldn't see that table yet, but if anyone could transform a surfboard into something else, it was Dad.

"Want to help?" he asked.

I nodded and reached for some sandpaper. Then I got to work sanding in small circles, as if I were waxing up that old board to take her to the Break.

Dad and I don't talk while we work. It's kind of peace-ful just hanging out side by side—like surfers in a lineup, waiting on a wave. So I didn't tell Dad that Sofia had ignored me all day at school. Or that Mila had one-upped me again at cheer with her handsprings. What a show-off!

Show-off. Just thinking the word made me wince because of my fight with Sofia. *Had* I been showing off with my frontside air? The question kept running through my mind. I sanded harder, trying to erase it.

Beside me, Dad was singing along with the song on the radio. Woodworking in the garage is his happy place, like surfing at the Break is mine.

At least it used to be, I realized. Sofia and I hadn't surfed together in a couple of weeks. Lately, I'd spent a lot more time at the cheer gym than I had at the Break.

I stopped sanding, feeling a lump form in my throat.

When Dad glanced over with a questioning look in his eyes, I started sanding again. But with every stroke, I started to worry. Maybe, just like this old board under my fingertips, I was turning into something else.

Maybe I'd never *really* be a surfer girl again.

The Surfers Code

When I got home after school on Wednesday, Liam was in the kitchen, raiding the cookie jar. When he offered me one, I shook my head. Not even a snickerdoodle could save me now.

"What gives?" he asked, tilting his head.

I shrugged.

"Come on, Joss. I've never seen you turn down sugar." He sat down at the kitchen table and patted the chair next to him.

I slumped into the chair and let my words fly. I told him that Sofia and I were fighting and that we weren't entering the video contest anymore. "Not that it matters," I said with a sigh.

Liam took a swig of milk. "Why not? I thought you were dying to meet Tina Hart."

I shrugged. "I am, but she probably wouldn't want to meet me. She thinks surfers should be all in—one hundred percent. But I've sort of turned into . . . a cheerleader." I fought the urge to crawl under the table.

A smile flashed across Liam's face. "So you like cheer?"

My cheeks burned. "It's not so bad. I mean, it's not what I thought it would be. It's hard work, and I've learned some awesome skills. Reina is really nice. And I *love* the trampoline."

Liam shrugged. "So you don't think you can be a surfer *and* a cheerleader?"

I shook my head. "Sofia doesn't think so. Neither does Dylan. Or Mila, one of my cheer teammates. But I ... I'm just not sure what I think anymore." I slumped lower in my chair.

Liam waved his hand. "Joss, look at me." He says that when he wants to make sure I hear every word. "I'm all about surfing, right? But I also skateboard and play volleyball. Does that make me less of a surfer?"

"No."

"Right. And Dylan surfs too, but he's also a really good photographer and filmmaker. Does that make him less of a surfer?"

"No." I could see where he was going with this.

"And your friend Sofia can rip, but she's also an artist. Right?"

I nodded sadly, picturing Sofia's "friend-ship" art, with that sinking ship.

"Having different interests doesn't make you less *you*. Tina Hart says 'Be all in.' But I don't think she means 'Be

all surfer' or 'Be all cheerleader' *all* the time. She probably
means 'Be true to yourself.' Do what you love, and give
a hundred percent to what you're doing *right now*—whether
it's surfing or cheering or hanging with your Surf Sister."

Huh. I'd never thought about it like that.

"You can do and be more than one thing," said Liam.
"That's what makes you *you*."

I wasn't totally sure I believed him. "What if other people
tell me I can't?" I asked, picturing Sofia's stormy face.

He laughed. "Since when do you let other people tell
you what you can and can't do?"

I shrugged.

Liam cocked his head as if he were deep in thought.
Then he grabbed his phone and pulled up an image. "Do
you know what this is?" he asked, showing me a photo-
graph of a sign at the beach.

I recognized it right away. "The Surfers Code," I said.

He nodded. "And what's the first rule of the Surfers
Code?"

"Give respect to get respect."

"Right," said Liam. "If you want people to respect
you in the water, at cheer, or anywhere, try showing them
a little respect first—even when it's hard. If *you* know what
you want to do and be, other people will eventually respect
your choices, too."

That stuff about the Surfers Code made sense. But right now, Sofia and I weren't two surfers out on the waves. We were two best friends who weren't speaking. Our friendship was sinking—fast.

As Liam pushed away from the table, I asked him one more question. "Liam, do you think Sofia and I will be okay?"

He smiled. "I don't know, Joss. But I know you. You never give up. So if you want to fix things with Sofia, I know you'll give it everything you've got."

"One hundred percent?" I said, before he could.

He shook his head and smiled. "Maybe even more."

On Thursday morning, I waited at the corner of the playground, where I would see Sofia getting to school on her skateboard. It was the second-to-last day before summer vacation. I had to talk to her before the weekend. Before the video contest deadline. Before a whole summer of surfing at the Break. How could I look forward to any of that without my best friend?

I didn't know if she'd listen. But I had to try.

While I waited, I twisted my bracelet around my wrist for good luck. Then I finally saw Sofia, her dark hair spilling out of her helmet. She saw me, too, and almost veered the other way. Instead, she kicked up her board and started speedwalking toward the school entrance.

When I caught up with her, I spoke fast while I had the chance. "Sofia, I'm sorry. I know I let you down with the video. I should have helped you more with your art instead of being all about the frontside air."

I paused to let her speak, but she just played with the strap of her backpack.

So I stepped closer. "I guess I wanted Tina Hart to notice me and my trick, but you were right. I was showing off."

Was she going to nod or *anything*? Nope.

I steeled myself for what I wanted to say next. "I know you want me to quit cheer, but . . . I'm starting to really like it." I glanced at her out of the corner of my eye. "I wanted to tell you that, but I couldn't. It was like you didn't respect cheer—which made me feel like you didn't respect me. I wish you could be excited for me, but it seems like my doing cheer really bothers you."

She took a shaky breath and finally spoke. "I know what it's like to want your best friend to be excited about what you're doing, Joss. I wanted you to be excited about my beach art! Instead, you just seemed bored by it, like you couldn't wait to [*mumble, mumble*] your frontside air. Or get back to your friends at cheer."

Sofia was really talking now. The words poured out like scalding water from a faucet, and some of them burned.

"You were *all* about cheer," she said. "You left me alone at the Break with a bunch of boys. You stopped wearing your Surf Sister bracelet. I felt like you turned your back on me!"

I lifted my wrist to be sure she saw the bracelet—back where it belonged. "I didn't mean to," I said softly. "I just wanted to win the contest. That's all."

"Well, the video contest was my chance to meet Tina Hart, too," said Sofia. "To show her my art and how I want to protect the animals, just like her. But then when you couldn't get the frontside air, you [*mumble, mumble*]."

"Sofia, slow down," I said, trying to read her lips.

"You said our video didn't have to be perfect—like it didn't matter anymore. Like my art and the stuff I cared about didn't matter!"

My stomach clenched, and a tingle of realization ran from my head to my toes. Sofia thought I didn't respect her art, just like I thought she didn't respect cheer.

"I *love* your art," I said. "Especially the stop-motion idea. And we can still enter the contest, Sofia. We'll find a way to show Tina Hart your art, okay? We'll film it together. I'll help you more this time, I promise."

Sofia shook her head. "You don't need to."

"But I want to!"

She held up her hand. "You don't need to, because I already have lots of clips of my beach art."

"Wait. You do?"

She shrugged. "I did it on my own. What else was I supposed to do while you were at cheer pretty much every night of the week?"

I thought she was getting mad all over again, but then I saw a little twinkle in her eyes.

"We have lots of videos of my art, but we don't have any surf clips. Not good ones, anyway." She sighed.

The wheels in my brain started turning. "I know someone who has plenty of surf clips."

"Dylan?" asked Sofia.

I nodded. Maybe he didn't have clips of me mastering the frontside air, but like Sofia had said, the video wasn't supposed to be about me. It was supposed to be about the Break—or what we loved best about it.

I told Sofia my idea, crossing my fingers. "Dylan might be down a partner now that Nico is hurt." I felt a twinge of guilt, remembering the look on Nico's face right before I collided with him at the Break. "With your video clips and some of Dylan's, maybe we could still finish our video!"

"Work with the boys?" she asked, wrinkling her nose.

"Yes. But only because we have to." I grinned at her.

Sofia thought about it for a while, making me squirm. But when she finally smiled back, I knew we were going to be okay.

She gave me a fist bump. And a couple of butt bumps. And one more butt bump, just to make me laugh.

My Surf Sister was back. *Finally.*

We still had to convince Dylan to help us. But like Liam said, I'm no quitter.

When I found out Dylan was having Nico over Friday night, Sofia and I set our plan into motion. She skated home with me after school, and we ambushed Dylan and Nico in the backyard, where they were playing with Murph.

Give respect to get respect, I told myself. Dylan hadn't exactly been nice to me after what I'd done to Nico at the Break. But maybe I could make things better.

Before we'd even crossed the yard, I could see the bandage on Nico's ankle. The fin chop must have been deep. Shame pricked the back of my neck, but I kept walking. "How's your ankle, Nico?" I asked, sitting in the grass beside Murph.

He grinned. "It's feeling okay. I'm tough." He flexed his bicep, as if to prove it.

"His ankle is fine," said Dylan. "He just likes the attention he's getting from the ladies."

Nico nodded and batted his eyelashes at me. I wanted to laugh, but there was something I had to say—something I wanted to be sure Nico heard.

"I'm sorry I dropped in on your wave," I told him. "I guess I was tired of people telling me I couldn't do the frontside air. But I should have been way more careful. I'm really sorry."

He waved his hand as if the accident were ancient history.

I took a deep breath. "I was also tired of people telling me what I could and couldn't be. Like I'm a surfer, but I'm a cheerleader, too." I said that last part to Dylan *and* to Sofia. "If you could see what cheerleaders do at the gym, you'd respect me instead of making fun of me."

Sofia's eyes dropped to the grass. But Dylan called my bluff. "All right, cheer girl," he said. "Show me what you've got." He waved his arm across the yard as if it were a tumbling track.

Here? Our backyard is tiny, and the ground is rocky. But I never back down from a challenge. Not when it's coming from Dylan—and when so much is riding on it.

I handed Murph's leash to Dylan so she wouldn't get in the way. Then I warmed up with a few cartwheels and roundoffs. I landed three back walkovers in a row, so fast that they felt like handsprings! Then I did a hurdler jump. And a pike jump. And two toe touches, just so Dylan would see how high I could get.

When I finished, I was breathing hard. But I struck a tight pose: one fist on my hip, one fist in the air, and a whole lot of attitude.

"Whoa," said Sofia, her eyes wide. "You're crazy good!"

"Sick tricks!" said Nico.

Dylan paid me the ultimate compliment. "Do that again," he said, pulling out his phone. "I gotta film it this time!"

"Not now," I said, trying to catch my breath. "I don't need you to film me doing cheer, but I do need your help with the surf video. I know you and Nico have your own thing going on, but … would you guys want to team up with Sofia and me? With your video skills and Sofia's art, we could come up with something really cool!"

Dylan rubbed his chin the way Dad does when he's deep in thought. He whispered back and forth with Nico, taking his sweet time. Then he said, "Sure. Why not? My video with Nico has kind of been on hold since, you know, he collided with some crazy girl at the Break."

I laughed out loud. "Yeah, I heard about that."

Never in a gazillion years did I think Sofia and I would be teaming up with the boys for a contest. But now, I couldn't wait to get started.

I didn't get any quiet time in my room Friday night. Instead, I got a different type of QT: lots of quality time with my Surf Sister and my brother. We sat in Dylan's room, weaving together his video clips with Sofia's. When Mom knocked on the door to say it was getting late, we were almost done with a rough edit. "Just five more minutes!" I pleaded.

"Five minutes." Mom smiled as she closed the door. I think she was just happy to see me and Dylan getting along for a change.

We all watched the rough edit together. It was so good! But at the end Sofia sat up straight and shook her head. "It's missing something."

"Seriously?" Dylan groaned, covering his face with his hands.

"The frontside air," Sofia announced. "That's what's missing."

Now it was my turn to groan. "Come on, Sofia. Forget

about the frontside air. I can't do it!"

Sofia stuck her face in mine. "Jocelyn Elizabeth Kendrick. Take that back. You *can* do the frontside air. And you're going to try again tomorrow at the Break. Got it?"

There was no arguing with Sofia when she was being sassy. "Got it," I said with a grin.

As I fell asleep that night with my Surf Sister snoozing beside me, I realized something: What I loved most about the Break was *not* learning new tricks. It was hanging out with Sofia, and even Dylan and Nico.

Surfing together and laughing together was what I loved most about the Break—just having fun and being ourselves. One hundred percent.

And *that* was what I wanted to protect.

Never turn your back on the ocean, I thought to myself. *And never, ever turn your back on your friends.*

The Victory Air

Saturday morning, as I waited for my perfect wave, I felt strong and steady. Maybe it was because I was wearing my Surf Sister bracelet *and* my cheer bow. And so far no one had laughed me out of the lineup.

I knew that wearing a bow didn't make me a cheerleader. And wearing my Surf Sister bracelet didn't make me a surfer. I was both of those things, no matter what I wore on the outside. But it felt good to have them as reminders—and to wear them both at the same time for a change.

Now I can just do my thing, I told myself. *Both of my things.*

When I finally went up for that frontside air, I didn't think about it. I let my body do what my body wanted to do, just like I'd been doing during open gym at cheer.

And what my body did was a tuck jump.

Instead of reaching for the edge of my board, I raised my arms overhead in a high V.

Huh?

When I realized what I was doing, I laughed out loud—but I didn't pull my arms down. I just went with it. I flew sky-high, like a superhero.

Then I was heading back down toward the water. *Yikes!*

I bailed and plunged into the wave.

As I paddled back to shore, I waited for Dylan to make fun of my high V arms. But he didn't. He gave me a thumbs-up and showed me the film clip.

I hadn't landed the trick—not even close. But with my arms raised toward the sky, I looked pretty tough. Even Sofia said so.

"I think cheer *has* made your surf tricks better," she said after I put my hearing aid in. "And maybe I am a little jealous." She gave me a sheepish smile.

"Really?" I pulled her into a sideways hug.

"So should we put your victory air in our video?" she asked.

Victory air? Ha!

It wasn't a frontside air, that was for sure. And when Tina Hart saw the video, she'd see me doing some weird cheer jump with a bow in my hair.

But when Dylan urged me to let him put it in the video, I said yes.

Huntington Beach hosts outdoor movie nights during the summer, when you can sit on the beach and watch movies on an inflatable screen. But tonight, Dylan, Sofia, and I were hosting our own movie night.

"Who wants a blanket?" called Liam from inside the surf bus. He had already set up a movie projector, and any minute now, our surf video would appear on the big screen—or on the side of the board shop. Reina and Ms. Goto hurried out of the board shop to join us for our "movie premiere," too.

Finally, Liam looked my way. "Ready?" he asked.

"Ready," I said. But I almost couldn't watch. I knew our video was good, but would it be good enough?

Dylan had edited in an opening title: "What We Love About Surfing the Break."

In the first scene, the word FRIEND appeared letter by letter with sticks, followed by Sofia's "ship" of shells. Then the video cut to a clip of Sofia and me doing our fist bump–butt bump–butt bump routine on the beach.

Next, the word COURAGE appeared inside Sofia's leaping dolphin. The video cut to Dylan's barrel ride, knobby knees and all, plus one of Nico's epic wipeouts.

Then came RESPECT, spelled out beneath a beach-art turtle. Sofia had filled in the turtle's shell with a patchwork of plastic pieces. Then we saw clips of us picking up trash on the beach, in super fast motion. *Ha!*

FUN appeared inside Sofia's seal, playing with its bottle-cap ball. There was a clip of me dancing on the beach at the Break—before I had realized that Dylan was filming me. And there was Murph, riding a wave toward shore. Everyone laughed, just like I knew they would. And then?

We saw TRYING NEW THINGS written in a surfboard below Sofia's surfing bird. And the video cut to Nico doing his crazy headstand on a surfboard. And then to *me*.

I held my breath, watching my tuck jump on the trampoline at cheer—the video Reina had filmed. Thanks to Dylan's editing skills, that clip morphed into the victory air trick I'd invented yesterday at the Break. It looked awesome! Even if I didn't quite land it.

A string of words suddenly appeared in the sand: BEING 100% TRUE TO OURSELVES. Sofia had used bottle cap rings for the zeroes.

It had taken us eons to figure out which video clip to use for those words, but Dylan had come up with the best idea. He'd added a freeze-frame of all four of us standing on a longboard in the water—the one Dad hadn't turned into a picnic table quite yet. Liam had taken the shot, and Dylan added arrows pointing out the "cast and crew": Dylan as filmmaker, Nico as stuntman, Sofia as artist, and me as surfer-cheer girl.

When the video unfroze, we all tumbled into the water, laughing. Then we saw the back of Murph's head as she doggy-paddled out to be with us, along with the caption, "No sea animals were harmed in the making of this video."

"Leave the audience laughing," Dylan had said. And they were. Liam whistled, and Ms. Goto waved her hands in the air.

The final frame read, "Help us respect and protect our favorite surf spot at Huntington Beach!" Everyone cheered.

Then I cleared my throat. "So I guess there's only one thing left to do."

We crowded around Dylan's laptop. He had carefully attached the video to an email. Then all together, we pressed SEND.

Monday night at cheer, I was a ball of nervous energy. Sofia and I had been counting down to Saturday, International Surfing Day, when the contest winners would be announced. Only five days to go!

I had to stop thinking about it, or I was going to explode. So I tried to focus on my handsprings. Now that I'd decided to stick with cheer, I wanted to learn how to do them. But it was going to take a whole lot of work to figure those out.

As I got in line behind Mila, I suddenly had a wacky idea: Maybe she could teach me! She was the only girl on the Junior Level One team who could do back handsprings. If I asked for pointers, would she give them to me? Or would she laugh in my face and walk away?

Give respect to get respect, I repeated to myself. I tapped Mila on the shoulder. "Your handsprings rock," I said matter-of-factly. "Maybe you could give me some tips."

She narrowed her eyes as if she thought I was messing with her. "You want help from me?" she said.

"Who else?" I said. "You're the best tumbler on our team."

As Brooklyn walked by, she whirled around, eyes wide. And Mila smiled—almost a real smile. Then she said something I never thought I'd hear. "I'll give you handspring tips if you give me tips on jumps. I mean, it's only fair."

Is she messing with me *now?* I wondered. Her expression said no. So I told her the truth about those jumps. "They're easier for me because I'm a surfer. If you really want to get better, you should take a few surf lessons."

Mila wrinkled her nose. "Um, no thanks," she said, before turning back to the mat. She was probably afraid that if she got anywhere near a surfboard, she'd turn into a damp, sandy mess. I almost laughed out loud picturing her ponytail plastered to her face with salt water.

We surfers are grungy sometimes, I wanted to say to Mila. *But we're a whole lot more than that.*

Could I change her mind about surfing the way I'd changed Dylan's and Sofia's minds about cheer? Not today. But maybe someday.

I'd keep working at it, like those handsprings.

One Hundred Percent

I hoisted a bucketful of trash off the ground and scanned the beach, looking for Tina Hart. I saw Mom and Dad by the lifeguard tower. And Dylan lifting a bucket, his legs shaking as if the load were way too heavy. *He'll do anything to get out of hard work*, I thought with a chuckle.

Tina Hart was here at the pier, too, somewhere. She'd be announcing the video contest winners after the beach clean-up. Just thinking about meeting her made my hands sweat.

Beside me, Sofia pulled a pair of broken sunglasses from the sand. She brushed them clean with her gloved hands and tossed them into her bag.

Broken beach shovels. Toy truck tires. Bottle caps. Straws. Plastic knives, forks, and spoons. Any plastic we found went into a separate bag, because people from the art center were coming to pick it up this afternoon.

"What is the art center doing with all this plastic again?" I asked Sofia.

Her eyes lit up. "Making giant sculptures to show how much plastic pollution is in the water and on our beaches. It's going to be a crazy cool exhibit."

"So . . . kind of like your beach art?" I asked.

She grinned. "Yeah, I guess so."

In the last few days, I must have told Sofia a gazillion times how amazing her beach art had looked in our video. And I knew Tina Hart was going to love it, too.

I checked the time on my phone. The contest winners wouldn't be announced until noon. Could I wait that long?

I hoped we'd get some surfing in before then. *But not quite yet*, I told myself. Sofia was walking farther down the beach, on a mission to clean up the coast—one piece of plastic at a time.

And I, her Surf Sister, was going to help.

Sofia and I raced into the waves together, carrying our boards. But paddling out near the pier was a lot harder than at the Break. These were the kind of waves that made a surfer pay attention, the kind that reminded us that the ocean was in charge—always.

As the waves pummeled me, I duck-dove over and over again until I finally made it out to the lineup. Dylan was already waiting there.

I searched for Sofia behind me. Was she okay? She gave me a thumbs-up.

When the next wave came, I waited for Dylan to go for it. I'd learned my lesson about dropping in on someone else's wave with Nico. But Dylan didn't take it. He pointed to me and grinned.

Seriously?

"Yes!" I signed. "Thank you." Then I paddled my heart out.

As soon as I stood up on the wave, my heart pounded— partly because of the power of the wave and partly because I was imagining Tina Hart onshore. I'd pictured her dozens of times during QT. But this time was different. Because she was actually here, somewhere in the crowd. She could even be watching me right now.

When I got the chance to fly, I was all in. One hundred percent. *Kick your board down, Joss. Tuck your knees. Scope out your landing. Can you see it? Now, snap your legs back down. Quick!*

When my board landed back on the wave, it jolted me awake—as if I'd only been visualizing the trick and now realized I had actually *done* it. I nearly wiped out with shock, catching my balance at the last minute.

I'd actually landed a frontside air!

My body tingled from head to toe, but my legs stayed strong. I rode out the wave for as long as I could, not wanting the moment to end.

Dylan hadn't caught the trick on video—he was out here in the waves with me. And Tina Hart wouldn't be seeing it in our contest video. It was too late for that.

But suddenly, I didn't care.

As the wave closed out, I jumped off my board—raising my arms in a high V for victory.

When the emcee announced that the winners of the video contest would be declared soon, I still hadn't seen Tina Hart. Was she even here?

Then the crowd went wild. I grabbed Sofia's arm and stretched my neck, trying to see.

"Over there!" Sofia pointed.

Tina Hart was walking onstage. She looked shorter than I expected and so *normal* in her T-shirt, shorts, and ponytail. But when she waved at the crowd, I swear she looked right at me. It was as if my poster had come to life! Even Dylan looked impressed. He'd been joking around with Nico, but as soon as Tina stepped onstage, he shut right up.

I heard Tina introduce herself, but every word after that was lost behind the cheers of the crowd. I was counting on Sofia to fill me in.

"She's talking about the beach cleanup," said Sofia.

"She says that [*mumble, mumble*] million tons of plastic are dumped in the ocean every year."

"A *million*?" I asked.

Sofia turned to face me so I could hear her. "*Eight* million," she said solemnly.

Suddenly the crowd burst into another round of applause, and Sofia started bouncing on her toes. She turned to face me. "This is it!" she shouted over the noise. "She's announcing the winners."

Sofia held up three fingers and cocked her head toward the stage. The third-place winners were being announced. I held my breath until she shook her head. "Not us."

Good! We didn't want third. We wanted first. We *needed* first!

As Sofia held up two fingers, my heart thudded in my ears.

I saw a teenage guy in the crowd start cheering. He'd won second place—not us. *Phew!* Relief trickled through my chest, then a pinch of worry. What if we *didn't* win?

When Sofia held up one finger, I could barely breathe. Or watch. I buried my face in her shoulder, because this was the moment that would either make my life or crush me like a bug.

It took forever before Sofia gave me a sign. She squeezed my hand so tight that I worried it might break off.

"We won!" she cried, pulling away so I could see her.

I heard Dylan let out a whoop, and then Tina Hart was waving us onto the stage.

Tina Hart. For real. My knees went weak.

Sofia tugged on my hand. "C'mon!"

I somehow made it up the stairs without tripping. I heard Tina Hart say something to Nico about courage. And did she ask Dylan about our bulldog? I couldn't hear every word—or even most of them. But suddenly I had something to say.

"Sofia did the beach art," I blurted, pushing my friend toward Tina. Heat rushed to my cheeks when she turned to face us.

"Well, Sofia," Tina said, "that art was really fantastic. I'd like to put it on my Save the Coast website. Would you [*mumble, mumble*]?" She was facing Sofia so I missed some of what she said, but Sofia's face told me everything I needed to know—she beamed as if she'd just won the lottery. *Yes!*

Then Tina said something to me that I didn't catch.

"Your aerial trick," Sofia repeated. "She saw it!"

Whoa. Tina had seen me pull off the frontside air? "I really wanted to do your move," I told her, my voice wobbly. "The one you did at the Break when you were my age."

Tina shook her head. "You did your own!" As she raised her arms overhead into a V, it dawned on me that she was talking about my victory air from the video.

"Joss is a cheerleader," Sofia explained. She actually sounded kind of proud.

Tina nodded. "I'm a dancer. That helps my surfing, too."

"You dance?" I asked, my jaw dropping.

"Sure!" said Tina. "It keeps me . . ." Her last words faded away as she twisted from side to side with a smile.

So even Tina Hart herself wasn't a hundred percent surfer girl. She was other things, too, just like me.

When Tina offered to sign our boards, I handed mine over. And in a few seconds flat, thanks to a permanent marker and Tina's loopy signature, my old board suddenly looked a whole lot cooler. I might have just won a new board, but I wouldn't be getting rid of my old one yet—or like *ever*. Maybe Dad could help me turn it into something new.

Then Tina asked me and my friends if we were ready to surf. "You want to teach me that air?" she asked me, raising her arms into a V.

Me? Teach Tina Hart my move?

My stomach clenched. I didn't know if I could stand up on a board right now, let alone do my victory air.

But Sofia was cheering me on from over Tina's shoulder, so I did what any surfer-cheer girl would do. I decided to give my all—one hundred percent—to this trick right now.

To my victory air with Tina Hart. ☙

🤙 SURF TERMS

AIR: another word for aerial, a trick where a surfer launches the surfboard into the air and lands back on the wave

CARVE: a turn on the face of a wave

CUTBACK: a sharp turn toward the breaking part of a wave

DROP IN: when a surfer catches a wave that another surfer is already riding; considered bad surfing etiquette

FIN CHOP: an injury caused by the fins of a surfboard

THE FLATS: the face, or flat part, of a breaking wave

FLOATER: a surf trick where the surfer rides the top of the wave, then drops back onto the wave's face

FRONTSIDE AIR: an aerial trick where a surfer pushes down the tail of the surfboard and launches it off the wave

GOOFY-FOOTED: a surfer who rides with the right foot forward

KOOK: a surfer—usually a beginner or someone unfamiliar with a local surf spot—who doesn't follow surf etiquette

LIP: the crest of a wave, where the water begins to break

MUSHY: used to describe a soft, unsurfable wave

OVER THE FALLS: a wipeout where the surfer free-falls from the top of the wave into the water

SNAP: a fast, sharp turn off the top of a wave

WHITE WATER: the frothy, churning water created by a wave

 *Cheer Terms*

HANDSPRING: an acrobatic move that involves springing forward or backward from a standing position onto the hands and then returning to the feet

HURDLER: a jump with one straight leg forward and the other bent beneath the body

PIKE JUMP: a jumping position in which the hips are bent at 90 degrees with the legs straight in front

TOE TOUCH: a straddle jump with the hands reaching toward the toes

TUCK JUMP: a jumping position in which the body is bent at the hips and the knees are pulled in tightly to the chest

TUMBLING: performing gymnastic or acrobatic skills on a mat

WALKOVER: an acrobatic move that involves bending backward or forward to place the hands on the ground, kicking the feet up and over, and returning to a standing position

 Other

EAR MOLD: the part of a hearing aid that has been made to fit inside the ear of someone with hearing loss

NOSE MANUAL: rolling on the front wheels of a skateboard

OLLIE: a skateboard jump performed by pushing the back foot down on the tail to launch the board into the air

Discussion Guide

1. At the beginning of the story, Joss holds certain beliefs about cheerleaders. How and why do her beliefs change? Have you ever changed your mind about someone or something after you learned more about them?

2. Why do you think Joss feels as though she can't be both a surfer and a cheerleader? Have you ever been torn between two passions?

3. Joss sometimes takes out her hearing aid for "QT," or quiet time. She does this to focus. Do you have a special way to focus or reflect? How does it help you get through the day?

4. The Surfers Code says you need to "give respect to gain respect." Do you think this is true? How do things change for Joss once she starts living by the Surfers Code?

ABOUT THE AUTHOR

Erin Falligant was a cheerleader, like Joss, when she was in high school. But unlike Joss, Erin had to work hard on her jumps. And while Joss dreams of meeting a famous surfer, Erin dreamed of meeting a famous author—long before she wrote her first book. She has now written more than thirty books for children, including contemporary fiction, historical fiction, advice books, and picture books. She has a master's degree in child clinical psychology and volunteers for the Madison Reading Project in her home state of Wisconsin.

READY TO FLY?

Visit **americangirl.com/play**
to discover more about Joss's world.

Learn how to be a healthy athlete in these
books, available in stores and online.
Each sold separately.

Parents, request a FREE catalogue at
americangirl.com/catalogue.

Sign up at **americangirl.com/email**
to receive the latest news and exclusive offers.